# HEART OF FIRE

## SEDONA VENEZ

Cover Model: Jacob Cooley & Nana Malone

Photographer: Wander Aquiar

WANT FREE SEDONA VENEZ
BOOKS?

Sign up for Sedona Venez's Newsletter and receive FREE BOOKS. In addition to the free stories, you will also get special pricing, exclusive previews and news of new releases.

**GET A FREE SEDONA VENEZ BOOK!**

Join Sedona's mailing list to be the first to know of new releases, free books, special prices and other author giveaways.

https://sedonavenez.com/free-book

# KENDRA

When I pulled up to my grandmother's house, I had to do a quick double check. Although I'd driven to her house probably a thousand times—maybe more—since I first learned to drive, it had been years since I'd seen the place.

I spotted the old pear tree next to my grandmother's battered old mailbox, shaped like a 1950s-era pickup truck. I'd never understood why Grandma insisted on keeping the mailbox —why she'd repaired and painted it again and again instead of ever replacing it, but it made it easy to find her house, set back a bit from the street. I maneuvered my SUV onto the driveway, feeling the cramp in my leg as I pressed harder on the brake. *Son of a bitch.*

I put the car in park and shut off the engine, taking a deep breath to steady myself. It had been weeks since my "officer-involved shooting incident." The wound was healed but had been severe. My bulletproof vest had caught the shot the perp had aimed at my chest, but my thigh still had a deep scar from the second shot he'd gotten off as my partner had knocked him down from behind. The physical therapist told me I could expect to get full function back, but I bet it would keep aching for the rest of my life, just a token of my service to the NYPD.

I got out of my vehicle and stretched my leg, hoping to ease the cramp along the scar tissue. I looked around me, and almost without thinking, my gaze went to a spot across the street. There was a house there, newer-looking than all the other ones on the block. Brick facade, little garden boxes in front of a bay window, stained-glass inset on the front door, white trim. I frowned, rubbing my leg, trying to work out the details of the house and why it looked so different from what my memory told me would be there.

It hit me all at once. The last time I'd seen the house on that plot, it was ablaze. Whoever had bought the property had just bulldozed the wreckage and built fresh, which was why it looked so out of place among the older homes on the block. The fire…

I stopped rubbing my leg, remembering that night and remembering the family that used to live in that house. More than the family, the kid they had. The first person to welcome me to the neighborhood when I'd been a sad, scared, thirteen-year-old who'd just lost her mom to cancer and never lived outside of the Bronx. The one who'd helped me navigate the suburban middle school Grandma enrolled me in, ripped out of the cramped, crowded, noisy New York Public School system. *Lukas.* I sighed and rubbed at my leg again.

I heard the screen door open with a creaky groan and turned to see Grandma coming out of the house.

"Hi, Grandma," I called out.

"Hey, baby girl," she returned with a huge smile.

Most people had mistaken Grandma for my mother when I was growing up, and even now, at seventy-five, she didn't look old enough to be a grandmother, much less the grandmother to a twenty-nine-year-old adult woman. Grandma only had a few strands of silver in her neatly braided hair, and while her ebony-hued skin had some wrinkles, they were what you'd expect on a woman of fifty-five, maybe sixty. Grandma had taught me her secret when I was a teenager—every day, she washed her face with black soap then smoothed on shea butter. She also drank eight glasses of water every single day, starting with a big glass first thing in the morning.

Grandma made her way down the walk to my SUV, pulling me in for a big hug. Clutching her back, I inhaled her familiar scent of lavender. *God, I missed her.*

Pulling away, Grandma pinched my cheek before stepping back and moving toward the rear of my SUV. "Open the back," Grandma ordered. I rolled my eyes before clicking it open, limping a bit as I tried to stop her from yanking out my luggage. I knew it wouldn't work—I would not talk her out of it, but I had to try.

"No, Grandma. I got it."

"You're a guest in this house, Kendra Powell," Grandma rebutted.

"And I'm your granddaughter. I used to live here," I countered, reaching for my suitcase.

"You haven't lived here in years," Grandma insisted. "That makes you a guest in my house."

"They're too heavy for you," I said, trying for another argument.

"And you with your injured leg—they're easy for you?" Grandma asked me, turning to pin me down with her gaze. I felt my cheeks warm up, and I sighed heavily.

"You take one, and I take one?" I suggested.

Grandma grinned. "That's fair."

I knew that although she looked like she was maybe sixty at most, Grandma wasn't as strong as she used to be. I let her grab the lighter of my two suitcases and took the heavier one for myself, balancing it against my bad leg for a second while I put my weight on my good leg before pressing the button to shut my liftgate.

"Are you going to get up the porch steps okay?" I asked, shoving my keys into my pocket and following behind her. Grandma nodded without so much as looking at me.

"The day I can't get up the steps is the day I get Martha

Peters's son Jackson to come and install a ramp," Grandma said. "And I will probably die a week after it's built, at that."

I snorted, sparing one last look at the new, pretty house on the block where there had been a burned-out husk before. I shook my head and continued up the driveway and onto the stone walk toward the front porch, trying not to think of Lukas. I stepped up onto the stairs, and my bad leg cramped up again, making me stumble. In an instant, Grandma had my suitcase out of my hand and her arm under me, holding me up and helping me onto the porch.

"I'm fine," I said.

Grandma tsked, shaking her head and letting me into the house. "You should have let me take that one," Grandma said, steering me through the front door and setting down my suitcase.

"I said I'm fine," I protested. "It's just a cramp."

"Uh-huh," Grandma said dryly. "Did they even clear you for lifting?"

I sighed. "They cleared me for everyday tasks and light chores," I told her. "I'm just not cleared for duty yet."

"And if it weren't my birthday, you'd be back in New York, in that tiny Brooklyn apartment, chomping at the bit to at least be on desk duty," Grandma said, picking up the heavier of my two suitcases and gesturing for me to take the lighter one.

I didn't want to discuss this thorny topic further. "Happy birthday, Grandma."

"Well, thank you, baby girl," Grandma returned warmly while propping my suitcase against the couch. She took the moment to kiss and hug me quickly, before bustling off toward my old room. "Are you able to keep up with me, or should I make two trips?" she asked me, glancing worriedly over her shoulder.

I hefted the lighter suitcase and followed her down the hall, to the room I'd lived in from eighteen until college, when I'd moved out for good. I followed her into my room, setting down my suitcase near the door. Grandma had changed nothing, other than occasionally cleaning the room and changing the bed linens since I'd last been in there. Missy Elliott posters, pictures of my friends from high school, and I could even still—barely—smell the horrible perfume I'd spilled on the carpet.

Knowing that Grandma was concerned about my well-being and recovery, I mumbled, "Grandma, my job is competitive. With being one of the very few black women to make detective, I have to work hard, take as many cases as possible."

"I know, I know," Grandma said, wiping her hands dramatically on her pants. "You had to make a name for yourself. I know my ambitious granddaughter. But all work and no play is a recipe for disaster." She eyed me. "I just want you to slow down, enjoy life, and take some time for you. And for goodness' sake, visit me more. I ain't getting any younger, baby girl."

She was right. I'd been going full throttle at work for so long that I'd forgotten what was important to me—my health, happiness, and Grandma, my only family. "Forgive me?" I asked, giving her my best doe-eyed look.

Grandma laughed and kissed me again, cupping my face in her hands and peering up into my eyes. "It's about time you slowed down, baby girl," Grandma said. "Maybe you'll get a taste for it."

"Maybe," I said while moving over to the bed and sitting down. "But my commanding officer back in the precinct is staying on top of any updates on my condition, my potential readiness to come back." Reaching down, I pulled off my sneakers, sighing while wiggling my toes.

Grandma shook her head. "You're still not listening to what I'm saying." Marching over to me, she plopped down beside me. "I'm proud of you and how much you've accomplished, but I haven't heard shit about your personal life." She pinched my cheek. "Like, when's the last time you were on a date? Or had sex?"

Grandma and I had a very candid relationship, so talking about sex wasn't awkward. "Too long," I grunted.

She laughed huskily. "So, I'm getting more action than my twenty-nine-year-old granddaughter."

"Sadly, yes." I hadn't had sex in over a year, and that hookup was fast and unsatisfying. Frankly, I missed sex, but I wanted more than meaningless fucking with some random dude. I didn't have time for dating. Besides, I intimidated most men because of my job in law enforcement. "But finding Mr. Right isn't easy."

"You're beautiful and smart. It can't be that hard," Grandma returned.

"That's easier said than done." I rolled my eyes. "My occupation brings a boatload of challenges to a romantic relationship. The mere act of trying to date is difficult. It's hard to find someone who wants to go out on a date with me when I get off at six in the morning." And sorting through all the physical and emotional issues my job brought into a new relationship was difficult for any man to deal with. "The dating struggle is real." I pulled my hat off my head and fluffed out my thick, curly, shoulder-length hair. "And the stereotypes of women in law enforcement are fucking ridiculous. Most men think I'm carrying a gun all the time and always eating donuts. There's a real lack of understanding of what I do daily."

Grandma snorted. "I'm not talking about dating some asshole. I'm talking about all the good men out there who will understand and respect what you bring to the table, baby girl." She paused. "Maybe you need to look for the right man in a smaller pool, like right here. There are lots of hot men in small towns."

"Lots?" I narrowed my eyes. "Here? I doubt it. The dating pool here dwindled when all the young people, like me, got the hell out of here, either after graduating from high school or college."

"Many people of the younger generation are moving back here in droves. It's refreshing that they're coming back to their roots to settle down. They've come to their senses and realized that the big city ain't where the action's at." She winked at me.

"If you say so," I answered. Unlike most occupations, police work often defined a person in the mind of a potential mate. There was an odd fascination with women in law enforcement. I didn't have the time or the patience to wade through that cesspool of crazy. Besides, it could be very intimidating for a man dating a female cop who carried a gun and had a legal authority to take a life.

Grandma grinned at me. "I say so." She patted my leg. "Enough about that. My party is tomorrow night, and you're here at least a week. I'll get the chance to fatten you up and make sure you're resting."

"I'm guessing your party is a big deal around here."

Grandma laughed, throwing her head back. "Baby girl, it is *the* party of the year. Down at the country club, lots of food, good people... I hope you're ready to see your grandma treated like the queen bee of the town."

"You've always been that," I pointed out.

"You're damn right I have, and it's about time this town recognized it," Grandma said. "I hope you have something pretty to wear for it."

"I have something appropriate," I told her.

Grandma gave me a little look—the look I'd gotten more than a few times living with her as a teenager, the look that told me she had a juicy secret she wasn't about to tell me.

"Good," Grandma said. "Because you never know who you'll meet."

I rolled my eyes. "Grandma, there've never been more than fifty thousand people in town," I pointed out. "My entire high school was less than the graduating class at PS iii. I can't meet anyone I haven't already met."

Grandma shrugged. "Still," she said while getting to her feet. "People come and go. You never know if Mr. Right will come strolling back into your life."

I frowned, watching her bustle out of my room. *What is she up to?*

## 2

## KENDRA

Grandma was right about her birthday party being the event of the year. The people who organized the event had gone all out at the Five Pines Country Club, putting up streamers in Grandma's favorite colors—pink and green—making sure the catering was on point, and getting a band and a DJ to cover the music for the night. I had to wonder just how much Grandma's friends had spent on the whole shindig, because given the number of people and the amount of food and alcohol, it had to be a group effort.

It had been years since I'd been in town, and Grandma was telling everyone I had come, sending them my way as she made her way around the area set up outside Five Pines for the party, talking a little to everybody. As I wandered around the party, I was stopped every few minutes, waylaid by someone I knew from high school or hadn't seen since I'd graduated from college.

"Oh my god, Kendra! How have you been?" Tracy Anderson called out, hugging me as tightly as she could, given she was sporting an enormous pregnant belly.

"Not too bad," I said, smiling and hugging her back. She and I had never been super close friends, but I'd always liked her pretty well.

Tracy released me, giving me a genuine, big smile. "Your

grandma is always telling us about how you're doing on the NYPD. How you made detective and all. I don't know how you get anything done—all those men in uniform?" She pretended to fan herself at so much heat.

I laughed huskily. "Trust me, when you see them gearing up or rushing to the bathroom after they made a bad choice on stakeout food, they're not so hot."

Tracy pouted teasingly. "Well, that's disappointing. Anyway... how long are you back in town for?"

I didn't know how many people Grandma had told about my incident and injury, but Tracy seemed to put a lot of weight into her question. "Haven't decided yet," I replied. "I'm on leave, but I should go for evaluations soon."

"Evaluations?" Tracy asked, frowning.

I took a deep breath. I knew I'd have to talk about it—at least a little—while I was staying with Grandma.

"Someone injured me in the line of duty," I said. "So, they want to make sure I'm all good before they put me back on the beat." I kept the emotion out of my voice.

"Oh no!" Tracy said, but I could tell she wasn't all that surprised at the news. I knew from experience that gossip traveled through this small town faster than the speed of light.

"It's part of the job," I countered. "But, hey." I grinned. "I'm in one piece, more or less."

"Well, I hope we can have time to catch up before you head back to the big city," Tracy said, reaching out to hug me again.

"Anytime," I said, hugging her back and finishing up the small talk before I kept it moving.

Ignoring the interested gazes of men as I moved through the crowd feeling sexy and confident in my all-black attire—a sleek silk blouse with a plunging neckline, paired with fitted pants that stressed my voluptuous ass. I had a thing for clothes, but given my long hours working undercover and trying not to stand out during assignments, it wasn't often I could wear the clothes I loved.

Grabbing a drink, I kept making the rounds, occasionally taking a break to dance a bit or to check in on Grandma. She was right in her element, living it up, talking to her old-lady friends, cutting loose on the dance floor. Ruth, Grandma's bestie for as long as I could remember, was dancing up a storm, and according to her, "Showing you young'uns how we used to do the damn thang." Grandma looked every inch the queen bee in her fitted purple dress, golden tiara, and silver birthday sash.

"Come on, Kendra, dance with us," some folks I'd known back in high school—invited with their parents and grandparents to the party—called out to me.

My leg was aching like crazy. I shook my head. "I'm taking a break."

"And she needs to get me a bottle of water," Grandma said, covering for me. "It's hot out here tonight!"

"Right on it, Grandma," I said, trying to hurry as much as possible to the bar. I didn't want to limp, but I also didn't want it to be obvious that I wasn't dancing for a reason. I waited patiently for one bartender to come to where I stood. I got a bottle of water and a glass of wine, and then I headed back to where Grandma was.

"Slow down on the wine drinking, baby girl," Grandma told me in a soft voice as she accepted the water from me. "You don't want to take a spill with your leg still so unsteady."

"Don't worry. I'm pacing myself," I promised before walking away to find a seat where I could rest for a bit without being too obvious about it. I relaxed, chatting with some of Grandma's older friends who weren't as robust as her.

Ruth walked over to me, taking a seat. "You look so good, Kendra." She smiled. "You know we're all proud of you, right?"

"Oh, I appreciate it," I replied, smiling at her.

"And you're a real beauty," Mabel, another one of Grandma's friends, said, leaning a bit into her chair. She had had a little more of the wine than she could handle, and her granddaughter was off getting her some food. "Why are you still single?"

"My job keeps me busy," I replied.

"Hogwash," Mabel countered. "You're a diamond. Any man in his right mind can see that from a mile away. Or maybe they're too stupid to recognize wife potential." She squinted at me. "Now, tell me what the men are like out there in the big city."

I shrugged. "They're the same as they are everywhere else."

Both old women laughed.

"I seem to recall that city men at least take some pride in their appearance," Ruth commented. "We used to go into New York for a week in the summer, and girl, let me tell you—"

Mabel interrupted her. "Oh, you can't tell her about that! She'll never believe that old women like us used to go pick up hot men."

I snorted into my glass of wine. "Considering some of Grandma's stories and warnings, I would absolutely believe it."

"Well, that was back in the day, when they were cracking down on marijuana," Ruth mused. "But you could still get 'special' cigarettes if you knew somebody in Harlem or Brooklyn."

I arched a brow. "Y'all got high?"

"Not like folks do today," Mabel told me. "You know, now that they made it legal here. I've been curious to see what it's like nowadays."

"It's still illegal down there in New York, right?" Ruth asked.

I nodded. "They started trying to pass a law to decriminalize it," I explained, "but it failed. They're still working on legalizing it."

"You know, I agree with legalizing it," Ruth said. "If you let people get drunk, you might as well let them get high."

I narrowed my eyes. "Well, I can't take a position. I've got to enforce the law."

Mabel gave me a shrewd look. "And then once it becomes legal, you can say what you want about it?"

I laughed and took a sip of my wine before saying, "When it becomes legal, we'll see."

I stayed a little while longer, chatting with Grandma's friends before my stomach began rumbling. Getting up, I started toward the food tables—it was a buffet, with some servers from the country club wandering around with other little bites and nibbles. Grabbing some chicken and a few pieces of fresh fruit, I gobbled it down.

Taking the last bite, I handed off my plate to a busser when I heard a sharp, loud crack. My heart pounded in my chest.

Three more quick, loud explosions pierced the air, and I nearly dropped to the ground on pure instinct. I glanced around for the source of the noise. The rational part of my brain knew it wasn't gunshots. I spotted the kids off to the side of the party, running away from the firecrackers they'd set off. Half a dozen more pops shattered the air, startling about half of the partiers—but no one reacted too badly. Except for me.

The firecrackers kept going off, and my heart raced.

Cold sweat trickled down the small of my back.

I shivered. The horrible memory of the feeling of the bullets hitting me came back in a rush. I brushed my trembling fingers against the leg where the bullet had torn into me. More pops cut through the air, making me want to run and scream. But I just stood there terrified, while hearing the echoes of my partner's shouts in my head.

"You okay, Kendra?" someone asked. I didn't even know or care who it was.

My voice shook when I replied, "Yeah, I'm okay." I had to get out of there before I made a bigger ass of myself. "I need to use the restroom. Be back in a second." I hurried back toward the inside of the building.

Once I got into the clubhouse, I made a beeline for the restrooms. I sighed with relief that the bathroom was quiet and empty. I went into a stall, closing my eyes and forcing myself to take deep, calming breaths like the department's shrink had taught me.

*I'm having a bad reaction.*

*It's normal for things to remind me of that day.*

*It's normal to not be okay yet.*

I breathed in through my nose and out through my mouth.

*One. Two. Three. Four. Five.*

*I am in a safe place.*

*The noise was fireworks.*

After a few minutes, my heart started to slow down, and some adrenaline evaporated out of my system. Walking out of the stall, I checked my face in the mirror. My amber skin was dewy, and my hazel eyes were a tad bit red. Pulling out blotting paper from my clutch, I pressed it to my face before applying more lip gloss to my full lips. As I took another deep breath, I smoothed down my hair before leaving the bathroom and walking back into the party.

"Here comes the cake!" Ruth called out from some corner of the celebration.

I made my way to Grandma, giving her a quick hug. A big commotion caught both our attention—a group of hunky firefighters carrying a large cake.

"Since there are *so many* candles on this," Mabel said, barely keeping in her laughter, "we thought it would be best to get the fire experts to bring it in."

I laughed along with everyone else as the group of firefighters brought the cake to Grandma. They'd decked out the cake in candles—I didn't envy whoever had been in charge of lighting all of them. The firefighters were hot, inspiring plenty of hoots and hollers from the tipsy women at the party.

As the men got closer, I recognized one or two of them from high school. A few of the guys in the group I didn't recognize at all. *They must have moved to town after I left.*

They presented the cake to Grandma for her to try to blow out all the candles, and my breath caught when I spotted him. The boy, now a gorgeous man, who had been my best friend until a fire had made him disappear from my life.

Lukas Koch.

## 3

## LUKAS

Seeing Kendra at her grandmother's side was enough of a shock that I had to make sure I didn't drop my corner of the cake. I held it together and pretended like I didn't even notice her, while Pearl Hornsby extinguished the candles in three quick blows. Pearl had donated to the fire department for years, so the chief had been on board with her friends' suggestion that we bring in the cake as a little joke.

"I'm just glad we didn't have to get out the hose," Blake, one of my friends in the department, joked.

"You better not have had them ready," Ruth called out. "We spent good money on that cake." Everyone laughed, and we set down the cake on the table someone had brought out specifically for it to let the servers cut and serve it all around. It was—as Ruth had pointed out—an expensive cake, made by a local bakery that Kendra's grandmother loved.

I tried not to be so obvious while watching Kendra taking her piece of cake. *Damn, she's beautiful.* Somehow, she looked exactly like she had back then and different, all at the same time. She was tall and curvy. Her jet-black hair was longer. Her face was a little rounder. *And fuck...*her full, pouty lips stirred up wicked, carnal thoughts.

The last time I'd seen Kendra, we had both been at the end of high school, technically adults but only just barely. Now, there was something sexy about her that hadn't been there when we'd been in school together—or maybe I just hadn't noticed it back then. Either way, she was definitely a woman, but she still looked like the fierce girl who'd frequently been in my corner.

Shaking myself out of my thoughts, I drifted away to get some food and a beer since I wasn't on the clock. I thought about talking to Kendra, but I couldn't make myself do it. *What would I even say?* I'd disappeared right after my mother's funeral, without even saying goodbye to Kendra or anyone else. Over the years since I'd been back in town, I'd made things right with most of the friends I'd had who were still around, but Kendra was the one person I desperately wanted to apologize to. *But would she forgive me?*

"Lukas, get over here," Pearl said, spotting me in the crowd. Kendra was right next to her. I grinned, making my way over in long strides.

"How's the cake, Mrs. Hornsby?" I asked.

Pearl laughed, shaking her head. "As good as any cake from Harlequin Bakery." She patted my arm. "Now that I got you over here, you and Kendra can catch up. Maybe you can talk her into staying for a good long while." Pearl moved away from Kendra's side faster than I would have thought possible for a seventy-five-year-old woman to do.

For a second, neither of us said anything. It was weird, seeing her again. I hadn't thought I'd ever really see Kendra after I first came back and heard she'd moved down to New York City. Her life in the city agreed with her.

"She's got a point, you know," I said, smiling.

Kendra laughed. "Yeah, I'm not sure she's ever even met subtlety. How long have you been back in town, Lukas?" She looked me over. "I guess probably a while now."

"A few years," I answered. "And you've been down in New York all this time, right?"

Kendra nodded. "Yes, I went to the NYPD after I finished my degree. Just recently worked my way up to detective."

"Congratulations. But you've always been smart, ambitious, and beautiful," I said.

"Thank you," she replied. "But it was hard work. I've made a lot of sacrifices to get the job."

"Let me guess." I arched a brow. "They surprised you when you got it, but no one else was?"

Kendra rolled her eyes, but she was grinning. "And you, Mr. Big Bad Firefighter. I never figured you'd be back in town. You could have at least called me—maybe I'd have visited sooner." She placed her hands on her hips.

"Work keeps me busy," I said. "But you know what that's like. I'm sure they keep you busy down there in the big city."

"Yes, very busy. There hasn't been too much time for anything but work," Kendra agreed.

I was smiling despite myself. Just being around her again reminded me of when I'd been in school. The good stuff—not the things I'd worked so hard to forget and put behind me. Around Kendra, there was that familiar feeling, something I hadn't felt with any of the women in the past.

"Not even dating?" I asked boldly. I wanted—no, needed—to know.

"No." Kendra shook her head. "But I finally have some time on my hands, so maybe it's time to change that." She winked at me saucily.

*Was she always this hot?* We'd only ever been friends, but with both of us grown up a bit...

The DJ changed the song, and I recognized it in an instant. Kendra groaned when she heard it too and looked around—I assumed to see if it was her grandmother who'd made the song request.

"It's a popular song," I pointed out.

Kendra laughed. "It's a decade old," she countered.

"It *is* 'our' song," I replied.

The opening of "Mr. Brightside" shifted into the first verse, and I held out my hand to her. "Come on. Let's do this."

"Hard pass," she answered before giving me a grin.

"Scared this German white boy could outdance you?"

She burst out laughing. "You couldn't in high school, and I doubt you can now."

"Then dance with me, Kendra Powell," I demanded.

Kendra raised an eyebrow then put her hand in mine. We moved to where more people were dancing and started moving to the beat of the music, just the way we had a decade before. But a decade before, we'd been on the verge of graduating high school, at the prom together as friends.

We sang along with the words; it wasn't possible not to. As we kept dancing, I noticed Kendra wasn't a little slower just because we were both closer to thirty than twenty. She moved, and I saw her wince. She was favoring one leg, putting all of her weight on the other in a way she never had when we'd been friends as kids. Maybe she'd fucked up her other knee in the line of duty, but she didn't act like someone dealing with an old injury. It looked like something I'd seen in the men I'd served with in the military when I was fresh out of high school and sent overseas by the US government.

The song ended, and I noticed Kendra was limping a bit as we headed back to where we'd been standing before our dance.

Moving a little closer to her, I said, "Here," offering her my arm to lean on.

She stopped, giving my arm the once-over. "Well, look at your Thor-like arm," she started. "I don't remember you having all this muscle potential in high school." Her lips tilted up at the corners as she teasingly touched the bulging muscles pressed against the material of my dress shirt. "Now stop being such a show-off. You're making the other men jealous."

I couldn't help the laughter that boomed out of me. "You're such a smartass." Pushing a stray curl behind her ear, I continued. "But this isn't about my spectacular guns. Just grab on to my arm."

Her eyes twinkled with laughter. "Okay, if you insist." She looped her arm over mine, pressing her luscious curves against my side.

Loving how good Kendra felt against me, I swallowed hard, tamping down my rising desire to push her into a corner, take her lips in a passionate kiss, and show her I was no longer the shy boy she once knew.

*Shit, Lukas. Get your head out of the gutter.*

I needed a distraction from my dirty thoughts, so I asked the next logical question on my mind. "I take it whatever happened to your leg isn't common knowledge?"

Kendra gave me the wry look I immediately recognized, and it was like nothing had changed in the ten years since I'd last seen her.

"It's not a fresh injury, but it's not fully healed," Kendra replied as I led her over to some chairs set up in the corner. She sat down and I followed, taking a seat in front of her.

"What happened?" I inquired. "Or do you not want to say?" Even though I knew good and damned well that Kendra Powell could take care of herself—I'd seen her in action well before she'd ever been a cop—someone had hurt her, and that was more than enough to rile up my protective instincts.

Her gaze darted away then back to me. "They call it an 'officer-involved shooting incident.'" She pressed her palms against the top of her thighs. "Someone injured me." She sighed heavily. "It'll heal. But for now, it's still stiff and achy."

"Did the bullet get you in the thigh?" I asked.

"Yes," she croaked. "It's one of those things—they give you a bulletproof vest to keep you from getting hit in the major organs, but your body's more than that."

I had to know more, so I pushed the line of conversation. "I knew a guy back in the day—different unit from mine but same division. He got some shrapnel in an IED attack, and they put him on PT." I paused. "They have you doing physical therapy, right?"

Kendra nodded. "Lots of it." Her lips twisted wryly. "The PT said I could expect to get seventy-five-percent function back. I'm supposed to continue doing it while I'm here since I know all the exercises."

"You'd better," I told her. "And if you want a workout buddy, I'm here for you."

"You look like you're no stranger to the gym," she mused while looking me over. There was a glint of appreciation in her eyes that made me want to preen like a peacock.

"Unfortunately, ever since I left the military, I don't work out as much as I used to. So, all this—" I flexed the muscles in my arms playfully "—is pure white-boy magic."

She chuckled. "Lukas, you're still crazy as ever."

I loved the way her face lit up when she laughed. I sat back a bit in my chair and grinned. "I see you still love wearing all black." I ran a finger across her knee.

Kendra laughed. "It's my signature color, even though Grandma is always whining about wanting to see me in something else besides black."

"In fairness to her, it's the truth," I chided. "Throughout high school, you wore nothing but black, even to prom." I smiled just remembering the battle Kendra had with her grandmother over what to wear to prom. Pearl told her that unless she wore a dress, Kendra wouldn't get to wear her mother's pearls to the dance. So, in typical Kendra fashion, she'd chosen a dress that looked as much like a tux as possible—black and white, with a bow in the front and tails at the back. It had looked hot on her, I'd had to admit.

Kendra rolled her eyes. "You two don't count with my clothes selection." She ran her fingers through her thick, shoulder-length hair.

"I'm not complaining, Kendra." Acting on instinct, I reached forward, tracing a finger across her cheek. "I bet you would look killer in something black, lace, and barely there."

"Just for the record, I do," she quipped before the tip of her tongue flicked out over her bottom lip for just a second. My cock jumped at the gesture, and my thoughts instantly went to all the dirty things I'd like her to do to my body with those full, pouty lips. *Jesus...this woman will be the death of me.*

I moved on to a way safer topic, one that would distract me from pulling her onto my lap and kissing her. "Why did you pick the NYPD over the FBI?" I asked. "You'd have the regulation FBI look down pat."

"I was thinking I might get into the FBI from the NYPD," Kendra said, extending her injured leg a bit and rubbing it discreetly. She was hurting, and just as obviously, she wanted to keep that to herself. My hands clenched as I pushed down my primal urge to drape her leg across my lap and massage it.

"Let me get you something to drink," I suggested. "You want water or something harder?"

"Another glass of wine," Kendra said. "That would be amazing."

I got up and hurried over to the bar. Since I was in semi-uniform, the bartender came over to me immediately. I got the glass of wine for Kendra and another gin and tonic for myself. "Who'd have ever thought we'd have a legal drink together," I said, handing off Kendra's wine and clinking my glass against hers. We both laughed, and I sat down.

"We weren't that bad," Kendra mused. "I think we only ever went to like two parties and got pissy drunk."

"We still broke the law," I pointed out jokingly. "What would the people you arrest think of you?"

Kendra snorted. "I wasn't a cop back then, and I didn't have any plans at that point to become one," she pointed out. "And you know it."

"I do," I admitted. "I have to think that, even now, plenty of kids break the law that way."

"They do," Kendra said. "Before I became a detective—when I was a beat cop—I must have broken up a dozen parties with underage kids."

I shot her a mock stern glare. "How many arrests, Detective Powell?"

"Cut it out, Firefighter Koch." Kendra shoved at my arm jokingly, just like she used to when we'd been kids.

"No avoiding the question, Kendra."

"Not that many," she said. "Mostly just made sure nobody would wreck anything or drive drunk, collected some fake IDs, told people to wait their turn to be legal."

"That's nice of you," I grinned.

Kendra shrugged. "Most of the time, the kids weren't doing anything that bad," she said. "Arresting them for being drunk or having alcohol wouldn't have accomplished anything."

"That didn't stop the police here," I countered.

"Yeah, but the police in a small town like this rarely have much more to take care of," Kendra replied.

I took a gulp of my drink. "Hey! I'll have you know there is plenty of crime here," I told her, pretending to be defensive.

"I can guarantee it's less than what happened on my beat," Kendra informed me.

"You should tell me about it sometime," I said before, from the corner of my eye, I caught my chief waving, wanting me to come over for group pictures to post online. "You're in town for a while, right? Not just leaving right after this?" I wanted to spend more time with her.

"Yes. I'll be around. My visit is kind of open-ended," she confirmed.

"Then we should get coffee sometime, catch up properly," I suggested. "I'd like to hear more about what you've been up to."

"I'm game," Kendra agreed. "I want all the stories of where the hell you went after high school."

I could see the questions in her eyes. There were so many things I wanted to tell her, like why I left town right after

Mom's funeral, telling no one where I was going or what I was doing.

"I'm off this Wednesday," I said. "We could meet up in town, maybe at Virgil's?"

Kendra's eyes widened. "Damn. That place is still open?"

"Hell yes. And still serving the best coffee cake in town," I told her. "So, Wednesday afternoon?"

"Okay."

"Your grandma has my number, I think—we have a directory for the elderly, with key phone numbers on it in case there's a non-fire emergency and they need help."

"Sounds good," Kendra said. "I'll get the number from Grandma, and we'll figure out a time."

I grinned and got up to go take pictures with the rest of the fire crew. "Look forward to it," I told her.

"Me too." Kendra winked at me, waving me off as I hauled ass before the chief could get annoyed with how long I was taking.

$$\mathcal{H} \quad 4 \quad \mathcal{H}$$

# KENDRA

I checked my face and hair in the mirror and threw on a robe before leaving my bedroom. I'd taken a long, hot bath infused with lavender-scented bath salts and done all of my usual evening skincare and hair care routine. And even though my leg was throbbing from how much I'd moved around during the party, my stomach was rumbling enough for me to want a late-night snack. I rubbed at the spot where the muscle still wasn't what it used to be, where the scar was, and continued on my way to the kitchen.

"Good to know I'm not the only one who got peckish," Grandma said from the kitchen table. She had our usual late-night snack out—cheese, apples, and salami, all of it sliced by her hand. *"Why would I get pre-sliced when I've got perfectly good knives at home and the hands to do it myself?"* she used to say any time I brought it up.

I sat down across from her and snagged a few pieces of local cheddar, two slices of salami, and a few wedges of apple to start with.

"So, was your party everything you hoped it would be?" I asked, taking a bite of apple and cheese.

"It was a damn fine party," Grandma replied, eating a slice of salami. "And it got even better when I noticed you dancing with Lukas."

I felt my cheeks warming up with a blush, and I rolled my eyes, getting up from the table to grab a bottle of sparkling water. "I didn't know he'd come back to town until he told me," I said, keeping my tone as casual as possible as I opened the refrigerator.

"Oh, he's been back a while," Grandma said.

"Want a bottle?" I asked. Grandma nodded. Reaching into the refrigerator, I grabbed two bottles then went to the cabinet for glasses. After making my way back, I placed the items on the table and sat down. "So, he's been back in town all this time, and you didn't think to tell me?" I poured water into the glasses.

Grandma shrugged. "You've been living up in the city. It didn't seem all that relevant." She took a sip of water.

"Are you kidding me?" I narrowed my eyes. "Lukas used to be my best friend, and then he disappeared…" I thought about the house across the street and the fire that destroyed it, killing Lukas's mother. I'd never found out about what really happened that night or how the fire started. All I knew was that Lukas's mother had died, and right after the funeral, he'd disappeared without even saying goodbye to me.

Grandma bit a piece of cheese. "The past is the past. We all have skeletons in the closet, and that doesn't make us bad. It just proves that we're human."

I shoved some salami into my mouth, mulling over Grandma's words.

"Lukas has a great reputation," Grandma told me. "Some folks thought after that…you know…incident that he'd be the firefighter who would end up freaking out in a fire." She drank some water. "It's a small town, so you know there was all kinds of talk. Some positive. Some negative. But our Lukas…"

"Our Lukas?" I raised a brow.

"Okay, your Lukas." She gave me an impish smile.

I ignored the butterflies that fluttered in my stomach. "He's not mine."

"Yet."

"Listen, Grandma—"

She interrupted me, "As I was saying...Lukas proved all the naysayers wrong. He's even got a few awards in the past few years for bravery. I always figured he took all the bad shit that happened to him and his family and decided he would never let that horror happen to anyone else again."

"Do you know what he did before he came back?" I asked, eating more salami and apple. "I mean..." I chewed and swallowed. "At the party, he talked about a friend getting hit by an IED, so I assume he's ex-military..."

"Yes. Army," Grandma said. "From what I hear, he spent some time in Iraq, and in the Philippines after that."

I sat back. "Wow." I tried to imagine the boy I'd known in high school in combat, fighting insurgents and terrorists halfway across the world from where I'd been going to college and then going into the academy. "Lukas's got to be one of the few people who came back more or less whole."

Grandma took a bite of cheese and followed it with a sip of water. "You know, given how things were in that house of his, I think nothing could scare him," Grandma mused.

"Well, that's a good point," I said, remembering Lukas's horrible father. "Did they ever..." I pressed my lips together, suddenly not so hungry for my snack. "Did they ever figure out what happened that night?"

Grandma shrugged. "Unfortunately, the case is closed, and no one in town knows shit about it." Grandma paused. "And that man who called himself a father and husband ran off before the police could question him. Near as anyone could ever find out, Lukas's father left the country. Rumor is that something went south that night and he started the fire, so if he ever shows his face anywhere, he's wanted for arson and murder."

"Jesus." I pushed down a shudder. I'd never liked Lukas's

father or the way his lecherous eyes would stalk me when Lukas and I would hang out on his porch. "Hopefully, the jackass slips up one day and gets his ass caught."

Grandma nodded. "That's what everyone around here is hoping for, too. One bad day and an extradition to stand trial for his crime."

"You know..." I twirled my glass. "The last time I saw Lukas was at the funeral for his mom." I remembered how skinny he looked in his oversized black suit with a white shirt. His green eyes were so cold and angry, but I'd wanted to hug him, tell him I was there for him. But I never got the chance... "I don't know." I swallowed hard over the old emotions. "Honestly, I was so hurt when he just up and left without saying goodbye to me."

"From what he's told me, that wasn't his fault," Grandma said. "The recruiter wanted him to ship out right away."

"Believe me, I get that he wanted to leave this town and all the bad shit as fast as possible, but..." I took a huge gulp of water. "Still, I wish he could have at least told me. I would have understood."

Grandma reached across the table, grabbing my hand. "Kendra. Sometimes when people are hurting bad, they don't think about others. They just want out of the trap. You can't blame him for wanting that, can you?"

I shook my head. "No, I don't blame him at all. I get it now." I knew how much it hurt to lose a mother, especially as suddenly as he did. When Mom died, I felt angry, abandoned, lost. And even years later, I missed her—hearing her voice, feeling her arms wrap around me when I needed her comforting warmth and assurance that everything would be all right. "In fact, he and I are going to get coffee, catch up a bit."

"Good." She patted my hand, then went back to eating. "I saw the two of you dancing," Grandma said, smiling in a way that told me she had definitely requested the song from the DJ.

"You requested that song." It was a statement not a question.

"Yup," Grandma said proudly. "I bet you never thought I'd

remember that's your song. But you sang it half the night after you and Lukas went to the prom. I'd never forget it." She paused. "Now that you're back together…"

"Grandma, don't get ahead of yourself," I warned. "Lukas and I are just meeting to catch up on our lives. That's all. So, don't start planning our wedding. Besides, we were only ever friends."

"Best friends," Grandma corrected me.

"What does that have to do with anything?" I protested.

"It's a foundation for more…"

"We're just friends," I countered. "And all I want is a chance to reconnect with a man I was friends with back in school. Nothing more."

"Give me a break," Grandma spat. "You're staying here in town for a while. What's the harm in seeing if there's something romantic between you two?"

I pointed at her. "No playing matchmaker. Lukas and I are just going to have a cup of coffee, while talking about work and where we've been in the world." I leaned forward. "And to be very clear, Lukas will not influence me one way or another whether I stay here."

"An old woman can hope," Grandma said.

I laughed, shaking my head. "You can hope all you want, but don't you dare fiddle around with my love life," I said. "Now, give me his phone number. He mentioned you'd have it."

"I sure do." Grandma got to her feet, making her way to the fridge. She plucked a thin, paperbound booklet from under a magnet. "You know…in my day, we called it a coffee date," Grandma said, handing the booklet over to me before she sat back down.

I rolled my eyes. "It isn't a date."

Grandma chuckled but said nothing.

I yawned. "I'm done eating." I arched a brow. "Do you need me to get you anything before I go back up?"

Grandma shook her head. "I'm just going to finish this apple and put the leftovers in the fridge. I need to get myself off to bed before I turn into a pumpkin."

I chuckled—it was one of her favorite sayings, one I'd heard a hundred times. "I'll put this back on the fridge in the morning," I told her, waving the booklet with contacts for the firefighters and EMTs in it around a bit.

When I rose to my feet, the scar on my leg twitched painfully. I'd overdone it a bit at the party. Sighing heavily, I decided I'd earned a dose of the Tramadol the doctors had given me for "as needed" relief, along with a quick rubdown with Mederma around my scar.

Once inside my room, I took my dose of medication, swallowing it down with my leftover water. Opening up my travel case, I snatched out a tube of Nurofen, then wiggled out of my sleep pants to get to my scar. Squeezing some gel out of the tube, I carefully rubbed it into my skin. My mind wandered back to the prom. We'd been just kids and had all the energy in the world. I'd asked him to go with me as a friend, because I knew he'd never ask me himself, and neither of us had dates. I could still remember the way Lukas's face flushed red when he told me about why he never dated any of the girls in our class, even though he'd been the hottest boy in the school back then. Plenty of girls had been so jealous of me for being so close to him.

"*I can't bring anyone home,*" Lukas said.

And that was true. I finished rubbing the Nurofen into my leg and stood up to wash my hands. Even before his father had burned down the house, Lukas's home was not a happy one— nowhere anyone in their right mind would want to bring a girlfriend, especially due to his father's erratic and often creepy behavior. I'd seen it firsthand, and Lukas had made me leave.

Drying off my hands, I went back into my bedroom, glancing around. It was the perfect picture of who I'd been years ago, not the woman I'd become. Life had changed for both of us; I just didn't know if the future included Lukas or not...

❧ *5* ❧

# LUKAS

I checked the time on the fire station computer then turned on my "away" message. Technically, I wasn't on call, but there was always the chance something big could happen, and if they needed me to muster up and get to a site, all they had to do was contact me on my phone and I'd be available.

I shoved my cell into my pocket. It was just coffee with Kendra; I shouldn't be so nervous, but I'd changed clothes a few times, looking for an outfit that was casual but good enough at the same time. I stared at my footwear options. I had several pairs of sneakers, boots, and an expensive pair of Italian dress shoes that I'd had custom made for me—given my large feet, it was easier than trying to find something in my size in any store. I wore my motorcycle boots. Once ready, I stormed out of the area, heading toward the exit.

"Koch!" I turned around to see Chief Mecklin coming out of his office. "You're on your way out?"

I replied without stopping. "Yeah, Chief. What's up?"

He hurried a bit to catch up with me. He was fit for a fifty-year-old, with a moustache that would look more appropriate on a seventies porn star. "We need a photographer to do the calendar," Chief said, matching my pace. "You said you'd look into it."

"I am," I promised him. "I'm looking through the options."

Every year, the fire department did a calendar with one of the local shelters, both to promote the shelter and to raise money for programs we kept going. The calendar was always a big hit and sold like hot cakes. Women loved half-naked firefighters posing with cats and dogs. But our usual photographer had passed away over the winter after battling pneumonia for a month, and we'd put off finding a replacement. But to get the calendars printed in time, we'd have to do the photo shoots soon.

"There can't be that many options, Lukas," Chief pointed out. "This town isn't that big."

"Stop worrying, Chief. I'll have some suggestions to you by the end of the week."

"Thanks." Chief Mecklin clapped me on the back before heading back to his office.

Exiting the building, I walked around to the parking lot at the back of the station and climbed onto my bike. It was one of maybe three parked by the station. Two guys drove trucks, one guy drove a sedan, but after years of armored transports, planes, and buses, I'd decided that if I could, I'd stick with something that gave me a little more airflow. So, with my first big paycheck after joining the fire rescue squad, I purchased a bike. I'd gotten it from a retired firefighter. He'd given me a decent price on the old girl, and with a little elbow grease, I'd kept her running smooth ever since.

Putting on my helmet, I took off, turning onto the main road through town, and headed for Virgil's, listening to the roar of my bike and the wind rushing past my ears through the helmet.

As I rode up the street, I thought about the photographer issue. The chief was counting on me to find someone. *Kendra used to take pictures, didn't she?* I remembered she'd won a few contests here and there back when we were in high school. She'd even told me a few times that she wanted to go pro one day, but I guess that never happened. *Maybe she'd be willing to do the calendar for us*. I grinned when I pictured Kendra taking photos of my half-naked friends. It would be funny, that was for sure.

Pulling into the parking lot Virgil's shared with a bait shop and a dry cleaner/tailor, I found a spot as close to the café as possible. It wasn't the usual rush time, so it would be fairly quiet inside. I looked around and then realized I did not know what kind of car Kendra would drive—but I doubted she'd be hauling her grandmother's jalopy around. I climbed off my bike, taking off my helmet and locking it to the bike. I headed around the front to Virgil's. The café had stood in the town for longer than I'd been alive, maybe even as far back as my grandparents' day. And even though Harlequin Bakery had some of the best cakes and pies in the town, Virgil's had the best coffee cake probably in the entire state.

I opened the door, and the little bells attached to it jingled. Glancing around, I spotted Kendra seated in a corner, talking to Lucia. They'd been friends in high school, not as close as Kendra and me but close the way girls are. Taking off my jacket, I walked to where Kendra sat. Both women looked up as I approached.

"Here he is...the gorgeous town hero!" Lucia yelled. "You want the usual, Lukas?" she asked, batting her eyelashes at me.

"Sure thing," I said, sitting down. "Double on the coffee cake. I've earned it this week."

Lucia licked her lips before responding with, "I'll just bet you did." She leaned forward to give me an obvious peek at her cleavage.

With amusement shining in her eyes, Kendra glanced from me to Lucia then back at me.

"Kendra, did you already order?" I frowned, wondering if I'd been late.

"No, I got here early, and Lucia and I got to talking." Kendra turned to eye Lucia. "Same thing Lukas's having, but half the coffee cake."

"Got it," Lucia said before walking away with too much sway in her hips.

Kendra laughed. "God. She's still crushing on you. It's like I never left."

"Things stay the same a lot in sleepy old towns," I agreed. When I'd come back to town, Lucia and a few other women had been very transparent with me—they wanted to fuck me. But I wasn't interested. I'd done my fair share of fucking around while I was in the military, and that shit got real old fast. At this stage in my life, I was looking for more than a quick fuck with a woman I had no interest in seeing in the morning.

"The perils of small towns," Kendra chirped. "It must be hell keeping hookups secret around here."

"I wouldn't know..." I said, settling into the old, reupholstered chair. "I gave up that hit-and-run life years ago. Now I'm looking for a woman to keep." I stared at her pointedly.

"Hmmm... Well..." Kendra's lips parted then closed.

"Oh, I meant to ask you, are you still doing photography? Or don't you have time since becoming a detective?"

Kendra blinked. "I still snap some photos from time to time. I can't believe you remembered that."

"Didn't you used to want to be the next Ansel Adams?" I asked.

"Not so much the landscapes," Kendra said. "More Annie Leibovitz."

"Right!" I said, nodding. "That was the one."

"Yes, I used to want to do that," Kendra confirmed. "I mean..." She bit her bottom lip before letting it go. "I still do photography. But it's kind of hard to get a leg up in that industry. And it's not any easier in New York. There's lots of competition."

"Well, if you're up for it, I've got a gig for you. We do an annual calendar, shirtless firefighters, cute puppies, kittens, and the occasional pot-bellied pig."

"You had me at shirtless firefighters." Kendra laughed. "Wait a minute," She snapped her fingers. "I think Grandma has a calendar like that in the kitchen. I didn't know I should look for your month!"

"I'm Mr. September. I posed with some adorable bunnies that we helped get adopted."

Kendra raised a brow. "With no shirt?"

I nodded.

"Well, I know what I'll be looking at when I get back to Grandma's house."

I grinned. "So, would you be interested in taking the job? I promised the chief I'd get us a new photographer."

"What happened to the old one?" Kendra asked, frowning.

"Passed away from pneumonia," I replied. "We'd be able to pay you for your work. Not a lot, but at least enough to justify spending the afternoon snapping photos of a bunch of shirtless dudes with dogs."

"I don't know...it's been a while since I've taken photos," Kendra said.

Before she could go on, Lucia bounced up to the table with our orders, coffee with double milk and no sugar and plenty of coffee cake.

"I'll leave the sugar for you, just in case," Lucia said, winking at me.

"The cake is plenty sweet," I told her, breaking off a piece with my fork and extending it to Kendra. "Try it." She opened her mouth, allowing me to feed her. "It's good, right?" She nodded while chewing, and I dove into the cake.

"Well..." Lucia's eyes shifted from me to Kendra. "The two of you look thick as thieves."

"Just catching up," Kendra said. "I needed to get all the news from Mr. September."

I nearly choked on my mouthful of cake.

Lucia asked, "Kendra, have you seen his picture? Whew," she said, fanning herself with a menu from the table. "Girl, the Army did him good."

I rolled my eyes while swallowing coffee.

"I can see that," Kendra replied, giving me a once-over. "He's all bulging muscles with a handsome face..." She batted her eyelashes. "I'm so proud of Thor the firefighter." She gave me an impish grin.

"Okay, enough, smartass." I shoved another forkful of cake into her mouth. "Maybe if we get Kendra to do this year's shoot, we can get some eye candy for the men of this town," I suggested. "Like a second calendar with the ladies of Wampanoag."

"There aren't all that many ladies in this town," Lucia pointed out.

"True enough, but I guarantee it'll sell," I said. "Especially if we feature Kendra as 'Ms. September,'" I finished with a waggle of my eyebrows.

"Not happening, Thor," Kendra grumbled.

"Y'all work out the logistics and get back to me," Lucia said before heading back to the counter to take care of another customer.

"You will not get me on the other side of the camera," Kendra said. "Lucia might do it, though. Maybe she can rope in some other women looking for husbands."

"But it's for charity." I gave her my best smile.

"Forget it." She pinched off a piece of cake and chomped on it.

"But I can handle your equipment," I said. "And I'll even let you wear a black swimsuit for the pic. We've got to show some skin."

Kendra laughed. "No way. If I do this—and I haven't fully decided yet—I am keeping my ass behind the camera."

"Fine, fine," I said. "But you'll do it, right?"

Kendra sipped her coffee and sighed happily. "I'll think about it," she said. "And it'll depend on when you need me to do it. I may not even be in town for that long."

My heart raced at the thought of her leaving town—and me.

"Did you have a set day to go back to New York?" I asked, keeping my voice as neutral as possible.

"Not exactly," Kendra said. "I've got some meetings I should go to, people to talk to...but nothing set in stone. They want to make sure I recover as much as possible before I decide."

I relaxed a little. "Sounds sensible," I agreed. "You need to know what you'll be working with, physically."

"Right," Kendra agreed. "They want to do a psych evaluation and all that, too. Make sure I haven't lost my mind."

"Well, in my unprofessional opinion, you're doing fine," I said, breaking off a chunk of the coffee cake and popping it into my mouth. "So, tell me all about your daring NYPD career."

Kendra chuckled and shook her head. "It's not all that daring. They have a saying about daring cops...they die young."

"You're a careful cop, then?"

"I guess."

I quirked a brow. "That doesn't seem like the Kendra Powell I knew."

"The Kendra Powell you knew was a kid," she answered. "They drilled into us in the academy it's better to know exactly what you're doing before you do it—on all fronts. You might have noticed the NYPD has gotten a lot of bad press in recent years."

"I wouldn't mention it," I said. "But I know there've got to be other good cops on the force, too. There're upright people in the PD here."

"I do my best," Kendra said. "But in a city like New York, we do a lot of community outreach. I wouldn't mind, at this point in my career, getting into that part of things more."

"Slowing down in your old age?" I teased.

"Are you?" Kendra replied, raising an eyebrow.

I popped another bite of the coffee cake into my mouth, chewed, and swallowed before saying, "Eat your cake, Powell."

"Stop asking me so many questions, and I will, Koch," Kendra countered. "Now, tell me about your Army heroics."

Leaning back in my chair, I eyed her. "Not so much on the heroics," I said. "I was just happy to get out in one piece—physically and mentally."

She reached over, weaving her fingers with mine. "Tell me about it anyway."

Tightening my hand around hers, I shifted in my chair and got ready to talk to the one person who understood me the most in the world.

❧ *6* ❧

## KENDRA

The café had gotten busier after Lucia had brought our coffee and cake, so Lukas and I had plenty of time to ourselves. But after talking about the kids we went to school with and where they ended up and about Lukas's time in the Army, both of us had finished our food and drink.

My eyes locked with Lukas's. "You know, I think I like this new, in-command Lukas," I said, sitting back a bit in my seat, taking in his authoritative posture and powerful presence. *Damn...he's sexy.*

"Oh, do you?" Lukas asked. Frankly, his rising eyebrow and questioning smirk made me hot. "You sure you don't prefer to be in control of everything? That'd be more like the girl I knew back in the day."

I checked my coffee mug, but there wasn't anything in it anymore. *How long had we been at Virgil's?*

"It isn't my fault I have yet to find someone I can trust to be in control," I said lightheartedly. His green eyes flashed brighter with something I couldn't identify.

One eyebrow quirked as he surveyed me with a tilt of his chiseled jaw. "Don't you trust me?"

My sex clenched just imagining all the sweaty, wicked things he was probably very good at in bed. *Shit. Am I thinking about fucking Lukas?*

"Lukas...I..."

Lucia stopped by the table. "We've got the Baptist bible study group coming in," she said, sounding apologetic. "I don't want to boot you, but we could really use the table."

I looked at Lukas. Technically, we'd only agreed to coffee together, and that was over with. The coffee date could end, and we could go back to whatever we'd been doing before we left to meet up at Virgil's. But I didn't want to just go back to Grandma's place and start rehab exercises or help her clean things around the house. I wanted more time with Lukas.

"We can go," Lukas said. "Let me pay, and we'll free up the table for you." He got up, keeping me from even making an offer to pay.

I sat at the table, waiting for him and trying to decide what to do next. I felt tingly all over—the first time I'd felt that way in years—and tense, but not the tension I got at work. It was the kind I got on a first date. It was crazy; I'd known Lukas for years, but it was like I was seeing him for the first time all over again. I watched Lukas pay for our orders and then turn around to come back.

When we'd been in high school together, he'd been this tall, pale, gangly, awkward kid with green eyes and black hair he'd kept long as a protest against his father. But the military had toned him up, and I couldn't help wondering what his broad shoulders and slim waist looked like under his T-shirt and jeans. I'd seen him naked before—but that had been on a skinny-dipping adventure when we were sophomores.

"Let's go for a walk," I suggested when Lukas came back to the table and gathered up his jacket. "It's nice out."

"And you don't want to go home just yet?" Lukas asked with a grin. "You can admit it."

I stood carefully, making sure I didn't put too much weight

on my bad leg. "I just don't want to clean Grandma's silverware," I told him. Lukas snickered.

"You up for a walk?" he asked quietly.

I nodded. "Marchman Park isn't far from here," I pointed out. "We can head that way, maybe claim one bench if my leg gets tired."

Lukas put his hand on the small of my back, and I felt that tingle again, that little burst of sexual spark. *What is wrong with me? Lukas is just a friend.*

*Yeah, but you haven't seen him in years, and he isn't the bean pole he used to be. He's hot.*

I'd known that, at least, in theory, back when we'd been friends, but it just hadn't connected for me despite how many girls wanted to get with him. It had connected over coffee when his green eyes collided with mine, and a welcome bolt of heat slammed into me in pure female appreciation. He had a little scar on his cheek from what he'd called "an incident" in Iraq, and it made him look manlier somehow.

He steered me through the crowded café and out onto the street. We were maybe three blocks away from the park, and it was still nice outside. Lukas grabbed my hand, and as soon as the ridges of his calluses slid across my skin and his fingers tightened on mine, a shiver of awareness shot through me. We made our way up the street toward the park, maybe a foot of space between us, and I realized that Lukas was keeping pace with me —slowing down to make sure I wouldn't have to limp to keep up.

"You know, I haven't seen Marchman Park since I've been back—not since the week I left," I said.

"We planted a bunch of new trees there this past spring," Lukas told me. "I think they've got plans to build a new playground at the other end—where the old one used to be."

"About time," I said, thinking about the old playground. "The old one can't be safe."

"They've cordoned it off until they finish the new one," Lukas said.

We kept walking, talking about town gossip, and after about two blocks, my leg spasmed. I cringed, and Lukas stopped, looking at me with worried eyes.

"It's okay," I said. "I can manage a short walk. I used to run a damn mile in eight minutes."

"You got shot," Lukas said. "Come on, grab on to my arm."

"Someone will see us," I pointed out. "Everyone will talk about it."

Lukas shrugged. "So?" he said. "Take my damn arm unless you'd rather they talk about me picking you up and carrying you around town."

I looked at him for a second and knew from the stubborn gleam in his eyes he wasn't joking. I took the arm he offered.

We walked the rest of the way to the park, and Lukas pointed out the trees they'd planted, which were finally setting in and getting themselves established in the summer heat.

"Hopefully there's enough time for them to flourish," I mused, reaching out to touch the new growth on one sapling. "In this part of the country, storms get intense by winter."

"The tree people said they'd be fine," Lukas said. We followed along the trail that looped around the park. "Hey, there's a bench," Lukas told me, pointing it out. "Let's sit down for a second."

"You covering for me or getting tired yourself?" I joked.

"It's such a nice day, I figured sitting in the park would be nice," Lukas said. "Besides, if you were hurting a block and a half ago, your leg can't be fine now."

I wanted to argue, but there was something in the way Lukas spoke that made me give in—willingly. I sat down, and Lukas sat down next to me, reaching out for my hand.

"You must really want the town's rumor mill to go crazy," I said, but I didn't take my hand back.

Lukas chuckled. "I don't mind if it does. They're already talking anyway, after we danced at the party." Lukas reached out and tweaked one of my curls.

"Are you flirting with me, Lukas Koch?" I asked him before giving him a wide grin.

"Well, Detective Powell," Lukas said, "what are you going to do about it if I am?"

I could feel my heart beating faster. "Let you have your wicked way with me…" I answered huskily.

"Right answer," he replied. "Tell me more about the NYPD." He didn't take my hand out of his, but he stopped playing with my hair, and I was almost disappointed. "I'm curious about that life. I almost went to the police academy after I got out."

"I'd been hoping to make my way up the ranks, eventually transfer to the FBI," I said. "Since I had a dual degree in psych and criminology, I figured it was a good career path."

"You figured? Plans have changed?" Lukas asked.

I shrugged. "I'm sort of rethinking my options now," I said. "I mean, it's not like the first time they have shot me, but mostly it's been a graze or the vest caught it—things like that."

"It must have been a serious injury," Lukas said.

I looked down at my lap. There were only a handful of people who knew how serious it had been—even Grandma hadn't gotten the full story out of me. She just knew I was in for a slow recovery.

"Can we not talk about that?" I asked.

Lukas nodded. "Tell me about your funniest bag," he said.

I thought about it for a few moments—there were lots of stories; anyone on the force in a city like New York had dozens. "An eighty-year-old drug dealer," I said. "Well, a drug dealer and nudist. We caught him in his meth lab, in an abandoned building, and he was cooking naked."

Lukas snorted. "Oh god, and that didn't traumatize you?"

I shook my head, laughing a little. "It was close," I said. "I'll never be able to look at Sudafed the same way again."

"Did you lock him up still naked?"

I shook my head. "No—thank god, we got him into a jumpsuit."

"How did you get him taken down?" Lukas wanted to know.

I explained the whole situation, which reminded me of another case, and we kept talking about the oddest cases I'd handled, laughing over the details together. I noticed Lukas was moving closer and closer to me, leaning in, and I didn't stop him —I didn't want to.

"Lukas!" a man yelled. "Chief said you were at Virgil's." I didn't recognize the man walking up to us. Lukas sat back, pulling slightly away from me but not releasing my hand.

"Sheriff Baker," Lukas said, nodding. "What can I do for you?"

Baker hadn't been a sheriff when I'd been in town last. He looked to be about sixty, graying, with the start of a beer gut, but otherwise in shape.

"I hate to interrupt your date," the sheriff said, glancing at me then back at Lukas. "But I was hoping to have time to talk to you about the youth intervention program. Chief said you'd be interested in helping."

"Definitely," Lukas said. "You guys have been doing good work."

"I also wanted to introduce myself," the sheriff said, turning to me. "You must be Kendra Powell. I was just starting here when you moved out of town."

I released Lukas's hand, extending it to Baker. "Nice to meet you." The sheriff shook my hand.

"Your grandmother has been talking you up a lot," Sheriff Baker said. "She mentioned you might be looking for an alternative to your job at the NYPD. And I've got to say, if you're looking for something a bit lower-intensity, I've got a deputy retiring soon, and we'd love to have you."

I smiled but made a mental note to tell Grandma to butt out of my career. "I haven't made any long-term decisions yet," I said, taking my hand back once it was polite to do so. "I'm still up for evaluations and all of that."

"But if you're interested, just know that we could use someone with your kind of experience and talent."

"Thank you, Sheriff," I said. "I'll keep it under advisement, for sure."

"We've got a case right now I could use your eyes on," the sheriff said. "Normally, we'd get outside law enforcement in..."

"That serious?" I asked. Despite myself, I couldn't help but be curious.

"String of B&Es," Sheriff Baker replied. "Not a lot to go on—usually in a small town like this, it's obvious who the suspects are, but here..."

"I might drop by and look at the evidence you've gathered so far, offer some insights," I said politely.

"I'd appreciate it," Sheriff Baker told me. "Anytime you're free—just as an outside opinion."

"Well," Lukas interjected. "If you can email me the stuff about the youth intervention program, I'd love to see it. I'll figure out how we can best offer support, what the scheduling will be like—all that."

"Right," Sheriff Baker said, nodding. "Like I said—I hate to interrupt your date, but I didn't know when I'd get a chance like this again. Enjoy this fine weather we're having." He shook my hand again and left, heading toward the other end of the park and the exits.

I looked at Lukas and laughed. "Date?"

"Yep. Date." He grinned.

"I forget just how subtle people are in this town," I said.

Lukas chuckled. "Well, you've got an alternative to your exciting NYPD career, if you want it," he pointed out.

"I do," I said, rolling my eyes slightly. "I mean, I guess it might not be the worst idea. Probably fewer shootouts here."

"You keep hedging on if you're going back," Lukas observed. "I take it the 'officer-involved shooting incident' was a little more intense than you're saying? Maybe you're not sure whether you want to go back to the job at all, even here?"

I thought about it for a second and then nodded. "I have some issues," I admitted. "I'm working through them. I don't really enjoy talking about it beyond that...but you know."

"Yeah, I get it," Lukas said. "I've got guys from back in the service—people I know—with issues. It takes time. No need to rush it."

"Do you want me to tell you about it?" I asked.

Lukas looked at me for a long few seconds. "You can tell me when you're ready." He leaned forward and pressed his forehead to mine. "Until then, it'll only make things awkward, right?"

I swallowed. His compassionate words were not what I had expected to hear. "Right." My voice was barely a whisper.

He reached up, cupped my face with his hands, and pressed his lips to mine. We stayed like that for a while before he finally pulled away, but he kept his hands on my cheeks. "I want you, Kendra. But I won't push if this is not what you want." He stroked my cheeks with his thumbs.

His words unlocked my last resolve. I kissed him. As I slid my hands around his waist, he slid his hands around my neck, wove his fingers into my curly hair, and tugged me closer. Lukas kissed me hungrily, greedily.

My body flooded with fire as I kissed him back, nipping his lips, tangling my tongue with his before finally pulling back, even though I didn't want to.

"That was something," I said, catching my breath.

Lukas licked his lips as if savoring my taste on his skin. "Damn, I've wanted to do that from the moment I saw you at the party," he said. "And you're a way better kisser than you were in the ninth grade."

"Oh, shut up," I said, smacking him on the shoulder. "That wasn't even the same thing at all. You just wanted to kiss a girl—any girl—to see what it was like."

"I've gotten practice since then," Lukas said. "I'd love to show you some tricks I've learned." He smiled secretively.

"I'm sure you would. But I think we've given the town enough to talk about."

"Well, how about you at my house, tomorrow night?" He took my hand, then joined our fingers together. "I'll cook us dinner. I'm a good cook, you know—comes from so much time dealing with fire."

A corner of my lip lifted. "Every firefighter I've ever met is a good cook. FDNY guys feed us sometimes."

"I'm better than FDNY," Lukas said. "And it'll give us some privacy."

My spine tingled, not just with arousal but with something baser, an appreciation for this flirty game we were playing. "I'd love to have dinner at your place tomorrow night." I looked him in the eyes. I knew what a date at his house meant, and it wasn't going to be just dinner and kissing. "Now, we should get going before someone else from town interrupts us with urgent news or a request."

Lukas chuckled, giving my hand a playful little squeeze. "You just don't want to risk me getting you hot and bothered in public."

"I have some self-control," I huffed mockingly. "And I have my dignity."

"We'll see how dignified you are tomorrow night," Lukas said, letting his voice drop a bit. "After you've tried my food."

"Are you that good?" I asked huskily.

"I'll let you decide for yourself, Detective Powell." He pulled me to my feet before we walked out of the park together, holding hands.

## 7

## LUKAS

I took a step back from the stove, looking at everything I had
going on. I'd started on dinner as soon as I'd gotten home and
cleaned up. The department had been doing a controlled burn to
prevent some fires later on in the season when it would get
scorching hot. And I'd come home covered in smoke, soot, and
dirt. Not the look I wanted for my date with Kendra.

Tonight, I'd gone simple with the rigatoni and a "Sunday
sauce" recipe I'd gotten off a friend in my unit back in the
Philippines. I'd gone out to the store the night before, after
Kendra had gone home, and picked up grass-fed beef shank and
Italian sausage, along with ground beef and veal for the meatballs. I had about half of what I needed in the pantry—pasta and
canned organic tomatoes—but I'd picked up some wine and the
fresh vegetables I'd need. I'd even stopped by the Harlequin
Bakery to get a fresh baguette to make garlic bread with.

The sauce was simmering away, with the meatballs ready to
go in, and the bread was in a warm oven, getting hot and buttery,
stuffed with so much garlic that a vampire would stay away from
both of us for weeks. The pasta would go on at the last minute,
and I had nothing to do but let things stay in a holding pattern
once I put in the meatballs.

I heard a knock at the door just after I got the meatballs in the sauce, and I hurried to get it. It could only be Kendra—there was no one else who might come over tonight—but I wanted to answer it quickly. The kiss the day before had left me tense, waiting for what would come next. I was in such a hurry, I didn't even take off the apron one guy at the firehouse had gotten me as a half-joking Secret Santa gift the year before. And when I opened the door and Kendra saw me, she burst out laughing.

"What?" I asked, looking down. The apron was useful, but I couldn't deny it looked ridiculous. On the front, it had the figure of a busty maid, with her tits and ass barely covered. "Hey, it's practical," I said, taking it off quickly.

"I believe you," Kendra said teasingly.

I let her into the house, and just as I closed the door, I grabbed her by the hand and pulled her close, kissing her on the lips. Just a quick kiss—I still had dinner to cook—but the feeling of her body pressed to mine, the taste of her lips, was enough to make me wish I didn't have to worry about anything else. I made myself pull back and guided Kendra into the kitchen, where dinner was in progress.

"Have a seat, Detective. I'll pour you a glass of wine." I paused. "I got us a Lambrusco and a heavier red to go with the meat."

"You really went all out on this," Kendra said, breathing deeply. She was in a button-down shirt and a pair of tight jeans that showed off how great her ass was.

"Just something simple," I remarked, pulling the foil off the top of the bottle. "A friend in my unit taught me the sauce— supposedly his grandma's recipe, but I suspect he held out on some secrets. Or maybe she did." Kendra chuckled, and I gave the sauce a quick stir before pouring the wine.

"If she's a real Italian grandma, she probably held it back," Kendra said. I handed her a glass of the sparkling red, and we clinked before taking our first sips.

"It's still good," I told her, "but not as good as the stuff she sent in a care package. I don't know how she figured it out, but she managed to get it through to him on base."

"It's probably an ingredient you couldn't get your hands on anyway," Kendra said, taking a sip. "Oh! This is good."

"I don't drink wine a lot, but if I drink it, it better be something good," I told her. "And according to my buddy, it has to be red wine with this meal."

Kendra took another sip from her glass. "It's not a bad Lambrusco."

"No, it's not," I said, turning my attention back to the food. I went to the fridge and got out some olives and other things to keep Kendra entertained while I finished dinner.

"When in the world did you learn to cook?" Kendra asked as I started the last stage of getting everything ready. I drained the pasta, set the meat from the sauce aside to eat as its course, and put the rigatoni in a big bowl to toss with the rich, tomato goodness.

"I learned in the Army," I said. "Honestly, I got to be a food nerd, weirdly enough. And when I was in the Philippines, there wasn't a lot of action, so I had time to hone my cooking skills."

"The Philippines is a good place to learn to cook," Kendra agreed before stabbing an olive with a toothpick and popping it into her mouth.

"I got a lot of practice, and then once I was back stateside, I sort of branched out," I clarified. I carried the food to the table and sat down, adding more wine to my glass and Kendra's. "Taste it."

"I already tasted the wine, Lukas," Kendra said saucily.

"You know what I mean, woman," I told her. "Taste the food."

"Such a bossy firefighter," she grumbled before taking a forkful of rigatoni and bringing it to her mouth. The lusty moan that escaped her lips as she tasted what I'd cooked was worth all the trouble and more. I tasted the pasta, and it was good enough to merit the reaction I'd gotten from Kendra.

"Damn. This is amazing," Kendra said once she had swallowed. "I can't even imagine what could make it better—whoever that grandma is, she has to be Italian magic."

I laughed and we both dove into our food and wine, just like at the café with the coffee and cake, talking between bites. We'd done our catching up, so instead of asking about careers and travel, we started talking about all of the ridiculous shit we'd gotten into as kids. It was good, thinking about that stuff—without rehashing the hell I'd gone through during the same years.

"Oh! I almost forgot," I said, "I have paperwork for you." I got up to retrieve the file folder the chief had given me before I'd left for the day. "It's the contracts and that kind of thing, for the photographer gig. If you're interested."

"I gave it more thought, and it sounds like fun," Kendra said. "I'll look over the paperwork, but I don't know if I have all the gear I need."

"Don't worry, we've got the gear," I told her. "Bob, the photographer we used to work with, left it to us in his will."

"That's handy!" Kendra exclaimed. "Could I have a little more pasta, please?"

"Sure, but leave room for the meat," I told her, adding a few scoops of pasta onto her plate.

It was dark outside by the time we finished, and Kendra gathered up the plates and carried them over to the sink.

"Hey!" I said, getting up to follow her. "You're a guest."

"You cooked," Kendra pointed out. "It's only fair that I help."

I grabbed a dish towel, letting Kendra take over the washing, and taking the plates and cups and everything else she passed me. It felt good, comfortable, and weirdly nice—washing dishes together, dividing it up, standing in my kitchen like we'd done a thousand times before.

"I'll put away the leftovers," I said. "After I've made you a plate to take home."

Kendra laughed. "You better."

I stepped behind her, putting my arms around her narrow waist. Pressing a kiss to the back of her neck, I breathed in her decadent feminine scent—a mix of lavender and vanilla.

I heard a shout from outside—the neighbors' kids—and then sharp, loud, popping sounds, firecrackers going off.

Kendra tensed in my arms. The glass fell from her hands, shattering against the sink.

She gasped then twisted around in my hold, like she was preparing to run.

"Whoa." Instinctively, I tightened my grip on her. "Are you okay?" I asked.

"No," Kendra replied in a breathy voice. "No. No. No." I tugged her against my chest, pressing my head against hers. She mentioned issues, she talked about an officer-involved shooting incident, but she hadn't given me any specifics. After years of working with guys in my unit and out of it, helping them deal with their trauma, I could tell at least a bit of what had happened. Kendra had PTSD.

"It's okay, baby," I said calmly. "I've got you. You're safe." She shivered as more of the neighbors' kids' firecrackers went off. With arms wrapped around her, I repeated comforting words— but the firecrackers stopped. I pulled back just enough to check her eyes, her face, to see how she was doing.

"I'm sorry," Kendra said. There were tears in her eyes, and she was still shaking.

"There's nothing to be sorry for, baby," I said. "Did you have a flashback?" Kendra nodded. I gave her another tight hug before guiding her carefully into my living room, letting her sit down.

"I broke your wineglass," Kendra whispered.

"Like I care," I told her. "Besides, I've been meaning to get new ones."

Kendra was still shaking, her hands trembling. "I'll be right back." I went into the kitchen to get her glass of wine. It didn't take long for me to bring it back to her.

"Do you want to know?" She took a sip of wine. "What happened, I mean."

"Only if you want to tell me," I said while sitting down next to her. "If you're not ready to talk about it, then you don't have to."

"I want to tell you," Kendra said, taking a deep breath. She looked steadier. "Just...just so you understand."

"Take your time, Kendra," I told her. "And stop if you want to at any point." I brushed my finger along her cheek.

She started, "It was pretty much typical. I mean, obviously, it didn't end up that way, but it was a simple apprehension. A raid. This guy...I tried to talk him down, get him to just put his gun down, but he was high on PCP."

"And he shot you?"

She bit her bottom lip. "It isn't even the shooting. I've had to have shrapnel taken out of my shoulder once. Usually, they instinctively shoot for the chest, forgetting we have vests."

"But he got your leg," I said.

Kendra nodded. "He caught me just...right where there's the big artery there," she said, looking down at her hands. "Before it loops up and goes to your groin, you know? It tore out part of the muscle, just ripped through me, and I almost bled out."

"You almost died." My heart raced at the knowledge I'd almost lost her. Reaching out, I took her hand in mine, giving it a quick squeeze. I had heard a dozen stories like hers, but that it was Kendra and not just another of my brothers-in-arms made it different. I could stay calm, but I still felt the urge to find whoever had done this to Kendra and beat the shit out of him.

Kendra carried on. "They could repair the artery, mostly patch me up. But ever since...it's like whenever I hear certain noises, I just lose it."

I remembered the party and the fireworks. "That happened at the birthday party too?"

"Yes. But nobody noticed. I made it to the bathroom," she

explained. "Got myself under control before anyone knew what was going on."

"That's fucking hard to do," I spoke. "I've known plenty of guys who can't manage that in a flashback."

"I couldn't let my issues ruin Grandma's birthday," Kendra revealed. "But this…this is a big part of why I'm not sure what I will do. I don't know if I can work through this enough to go back to the NYPD, or even to work as a cop here."

"I get it," I stated. "You don't have to decide right now. I won't pressure you—and I can talk to your grandma if she tries it."

Kendra laughed, and I knew she was fully over the worst of it. "Good luck with that."

She took a deep breath. "Do you want to see it?" Kendra invited. "I haven't even shown Grandma. Nobody but the doctors, really."

I kissed her softly before pulling back. "Show me."

Kendra placed her glass on my coffee table before taking off her boots and getting to her feet. She untied the sash at her waist then shimmied out of her jeans, standing before me in her panties—creamy white, with lace—and her button-down shirt. For a second, I didn't even look at her leg, and I just appreciated how fucking beautiful she was with her silky, dark skin and curvy hips.

Kendra locked eyes with me while turning her leg slightly. It was then I saw the scar tracking up from a little above her knee, right across the femoral artery. Leaning forward, I traced the scar lightly with the tip of my finger, knowing how sensitive it could be—I could tell why it was so painful. It wasn't as bad as some wounds I'd seen, but it marked her ebony-hued skin.

"It's horrible," Kendra declared, her voice light, but I could hear the pain in it too.

"Want to see something?" I asked her. I stood up before she could answer and started unbuttoning my shirt. Peeling it off and tossing it away, I stepped forward so Kendra could observe what I wanted her to see.

Her eyes widened. "That's from the Army?"

"No." I shook my head, pushing down the urge to shiver as Kendra's fingertips traced over the scars on my shoulders, back, and chest. They were halfway faded, but they still looked angry enough that I hated to see them. I hated for other people to see them too. "The night of the fire. Part of the roof collapsed when I was trying to get Mom out. I suffered second-degree burns and a few spots where it was third-degree."

"You... I didn't even know." Kendra frowned, looking up into my eyes. "You said nothing at the funeral. I didn't even know the fire had injured you."

"When I signed up for the Army, I was well enough to go to get my physical and all that," I said. "They put me up, gave me long enough to heal so I could do Basic. But that's not the point."

"Then what is?" Kendra rebutted.

I put my arms around her, looking down into her hazel eyes. "Your scar doesn't make you any less—not less beautiful, not less strong. You'll recover from this, and you'll keep going."

8

### KENDRA

Before I could say anything in response to Lukas, he leaned in and kissed me. I wrapped my arms around his shoulders, feeling warm and shockingly safe, considering the flashback I'd just had. As I pressed my body against his, Lukas deepened our kiss, letting his hands move over me. My cunt clenched when he dipped down from my lips to my neck, nibbling at my sensitive skin.

Slowly, I pulled back. "When did you become such a bad boy?"

"I've always been bad," he growled. "You just didn't know it." He tugged me closer. "Shirt off," he demanded.

My eyes widened at his boldness. "Damn. It's Dom Lukas." I winked at him. "Me likey."

"Good." He nipped my bottom lip. "Because I've waited a long time for you, Kendra Powell, and I'm planning on wearing your ass out tonight."

My pussy pulsed. "Sweet Jesus." This was way too good to be true. I was about to fuck the boy—now a gorgeous, caring man —I practically grew up with.

He stared at me with a serious expression. "But if you don't want this, just say so, and I'll stop right now." He clutched my face. "Kendra, this is all your call."

"There is no way this is not happening, Lukas." I unbuttoned my shirt, letting it fall to the floor. Then I unhooked my bra, tossing it over my shoulder.

He let out a haggard breath, his gaze dropping to my bared breasts. "God, you're so beautiful." Lukas wet his bottom lip. It was a look of such desire and hunger that my breath hitched. "Let's go to my bedroom."

I squealed when he picked me up effortlessly. Instinctively, I wrapped my legs around his lean waist as he carried me through his house, kicking open his bedroom door like he was the police.

Dropping me onto his bed, he straddled me, one knee on each side of my waist. I peered up at him with greedy anticipation. His firm lips curved up into a smile.

He cupped my cheek in one huge hand. "Do you trust me to take care of you?"

"Yes," I whispered.

In the blink of an eye, he hooked my legs over his shoulders. Settling himself between the V of my thighs, he pushed my panties aside before licking my cunt. I moaned when his tongue lapped me from my clit to the end of my cleft. He swirled his tongue around my clit, flicking it and sinking it inside me. I panted, my hips arching and my hands grabbing at the sheets.

"Who does this pussy belong to?" he gritted out as he fucked me with his wicked tongue.

"You!" I screamed.

His tongue flicked my swollen nub. "Oh my fucking god!" I screamed. "Please... I need... I want..."

Abruptly, he relented, pulling away. "What do you want?" His green eyes blazed with a focused, animal wildness.

"Fuck me," I demanded.

He growled before standing and stripping slowly. His skin was golden-colored and tight over bulging muscles beneath. He was, without a doubt, the sexiest man I'd ever seen. I dropped my eyes lower. His large erection was thick, hard, and jutting toward me. He was huge, and my mind raced, wondering how the hell he would fit all that inside me. I watched as he walked over to his bedside table, opening a drawer and taking out a condom. He tore open the package, quickly removing the latex and sheathing his cock.

He came back over to the bed, tugging off my panties, exposing me completely before joining me on the bed. Hovering right above me, he slowly buried himself inside me. He gave my wetness time to adjust to his girth.

"Relax," he hissed, but my hips bucked.

He held me still. "Slow, darling. You're tight, and I don't want to hurt you."

I took a deep breath, forcing my muscles to loosen. He pushed forward, slowly at first, and then he increased his speed from a sensuous slide to a hard, forceful pumping.

"Fuck," he cursed. "You're so tight."

He was driving me crazy with lust, each stroke bringing me closer and closer to the edge. In a million years, I never would have thought my best friend from school could turn me on like this.

"Lukas," I groaned as he continued to fuck me like a man possessed. His thrusts were short and fast. I groaned in pleasure, taking everything he had to give. Our slick bodies were in perfect synchronicity, a strange magnetic energy encircling us.

"Lukas, please." My body begged for sweet release.

With a low groan, he plunged into me before I felt the orgasm ripping up my spine, tearing through my limbs. Lukas spasmed inside me while shouting my name at the top of his lungs. He peered down at me with a sexy, bad-boy smile. "Damn," he hissed.

"Yes...damn," I replied.

Tremors ran through me as he trailed his lips across my shoulder before pushing the damp strands of hair away from my forehead.

"You know," I said, placing my hands on the sides of his face while stroking his jaw, staring into his green eyes. His lips curled up into a contented smile. I'd never seen anything more beautiful than Lukas. "If all my flashbacks had a happy ending like that, I'd be a lot less scared of them."

Lukas kissed me softly. "There's nothing like sex to take your mind off things," Lukas said, brushing my nipple with the backs of his knuckles.

"Hell yes," I said, wriggling underneath Lukas to get his weight where I wanted it. It was even better than the sex. Feeling his weight on me, his body pressed to mine, his cock—still wrapped in latex—twitching lightly inside of me. It felt safe, and I realized I hadn't really felt safe, down to my bones, since the incident, even at Grandma's house.

"And if you stay," Lukas said, holding himself up to look down into my eyes. "I could make this happen regularly."

I arched a brow. "Are you trying to bribe me with hot sex right now?"

"Uh-huh." He devoured my mouth with sweeping strokes of his tongue, slow and deep before breaking away and saying, "Now, tell me you'd give me, us, and you staying in town some..." A loud siren sound erupted from outside the bedroom. "Fuck!" he yelled while rolling off me quickly.

I watched him, wide-eyed. "What is that?" I asked, sitting up quickly, enjoying the sight of his toned, naked body. "Did you leave the stove on or something?" *Damn. He moves fast for a man the size of Thor.*

"No. It's the ringtone for work," he said, storming into his bathroom and leaving the door open. I heard him slamming things and the sound of water running. "I'm not on call formally." He peered out of the bathroom, eyeing me, with a washcloth in hand. The condom was now off his cock. "But something must have gone down where they need all hands on deck."

"Shit," I muttered, scrambling off the bed and snatching my panties from the floor.

He dipped back into the bathroom then hurried out just as I brushed past him, needing to use the bathroom. While inside taking care of business, I heard Lukas say, "Hey, Chief. What's up?" There was a beat of silence. I walked out of the bathroom to see Lukas dressed in a T-shirt and jeans, and with his cell pressed to his ear, still listening to the chief. I hurried past him, but he grabbed me, pressing a quick kiss to my lips before he replied into the phone, "Yeah. Got it. I can be there in fifteen." He ended the call, shoving his cell into his pocket before wrapping his arms around me.

He looked at me; I knew the look. It was one I'd worn a few times when work called me in during a date.

Peering up at him, I asked, "What's going on?"

"There was a B&E," he said. "And somehow, a fire started. There's not a lot of information just yet. But the fire is fucking huge."

"I'm coming with you," I replied. "It might be fun to watch Firefighter Lukas in action." I winked at him. "Then we can go back to the date afterward."

He grinned. "I hoped that you'd say that." He gave me a peck. "Let's go, Detective. We need to haul ass." He slapped my butt before releasing me.

I growled mischievously before saying, "Slap my ass again, and I'll show you how I subdue perps twice my size before hand-cuffing them."

"Now that's a thought," he growled huskily while clutching my hands and guiding me out of his bedroom to collect my clothes dropped in the living room. "Both of us nude while you try to handcuff me. Who knows, I might enjoy that."

I laughed loudly. "Kinky Lukas...behave."

## 9

## LUKAS

The team had the fire about halfway under control by the time I got there, and it only took me a minute to gear up and help take care of the rest of it.

The house would be a total loss. I didn't have to be an insurance adjuster to know that. Even just looking at the place in the dark, drenched in spotlights to help the crew, it was obvious. If the foundation hadn't cracked, it would be a miracle. It took us about thirty minutes to get the fire completely extinguished, and the family that lived in the place would have to hope their insurance would cover a hotel room for the night—though I knew that if they didn't have that kind of coverage, the chief would figure something out for them. But they would be effectively homeless. The family was standing off to the side, their dog—a Rhodesian ridgeback—positioned next to them, and they were talking to the cops.

I shucked my gear and went looking for Kendra as soon as the cops started documenting the scene. Kendra was talking with the sheriff, both of them looking at a stack of paperwork on the hood of the sheriff's cruiser. I smiled to myself, thinking that even if Kendra didn't think she was ready to be a cop again, she'd fallen into it naturally. I hadn't even suggested she do anything, other than stay out of the way, and she'd given me another of those looks—one that told me I would pay for it later.

Engrossed in her conversation with the sheriff, Kendra didn't spare me a glance when I approached.

"And you see that?" Kendra asked the sheriff, pointing to the items on the hood of his cruiser. "All the pictures of the crime scenes show that same distinctive mark."

"The real question is, what the hell is that from?" Sheriff Baker asked.

I hung back, letting Kendra have her conference with the sheriff, but listening in—and watching her. I'd always had the greatest respect for her, but observing her in a work setting, being all business, was a whole other thing. If I hadn't seen her reaction to the fireworks, I never would have thought she was the same person. The woman I now saw talking to the sheriff was sharp, insightful, and professional. Nobody who witnessed how she scrutinized the evidence, or who heard the questions she was asking, would think she was suffering from PTSD.

The sheriff looked up, spotting me, and waved me over. "Lukas. Kendra and I are just going over the evidence."

"Looking at all this, I'd say your suspicion is right," Kendra informed the sheriff. "We can link the B&Es to the same perp, and it follows a pattern...technically, an escalation."

"So, what's your estimation of what happened here?" I asked.

The sheriff scratched his chin. "According to the family, they were in the den at the back of the house when they heard a loud noise. The dog charged through the house, attacking the intruder in the kitchen."

"The family told us they had some extra kerosene for their heater stored in the kitchen," Kendra said. "So, the sheriff and I think the intruder used kerosene to set the fire that spread throughout the house."

I shook my head. "When will people realize it's not smart to store extra kerosene in the house?"

Kendra replied, "It's the simple things that people forget to do."

The sheriff pulled off his hat, rubbing his fingers through his hair, agitation written all over his face. "This is the tenth house this guy has hit, assuming it's the same person. He's taking small valuables, nothing so far that would net him enough to stop."

"And he's not leaving behind enough evidence so you can conclusively say who it is," Kendra surmised.

"That's about the shape of it," the sheriff confirmed. "If we had more people—more experienced people—to look into it..." He glanced over at Kendra.

She sighed heavily. "Look, Sheriff, I'm happy to consult but..."

"Sheriff," I interjected, "I don't think Kendra's even heard from the NYPD yet on when they expect her to come in for evaluation."

Kendra gave me a grateful look for stepping in at her hesitation.

The sheriff patted her shoulder. "It's already been a big help, having you look over what we've got. Believe me, I appreciate your insights."

"I'm happy to give them," Kendra responded with a smile.

The sheriff turned to me. "Since this is arson, it will involve the fire department on this one, I assume?"

I nodded. The chief was already getting to work alongside the cops. "Yeah, we'll be in on this case, at least. We'll share what evidence we've collected with the PD."

The sheriff gathered up his files. "I'd better get with the chief and see what we can do for these poor folks." He glanced over at the family then back to Kendra. "If you think of anything—or want more access to the file—I'm happy to talk anytime. Lukas has my cell number."

Kendra nodded her agreement to the invitation, and we watched the sheriff walk off to talk to the victims.

"Back to my place?" I asked Kendra as she took another look around the scene.

"Yes," Kendra agreed, turning her attention back to me. "I'm actually hungry for seconds."

"Seconds of what?" I grinned, taking her hand, walking back toward my bike.

Kendra gave me a sassy grin. "That delicious meal you made for me."

"That's all?" I asked, letting go of her hand, pushing her helmet and jacket toward her.

"Yes, that's all," she retorted, putting on her jacket then strapping on her helmet.

"I'm just saying…" I answered as I threw my leg over the bike and turned it on. "I'm good to go for—" I held up two fingers "—round two."

"I bet you are," she said before hopping onto the bike behind me and wrapping her arms around my waist tight enough to stay close.

I pushed backward, my ass coming into contact with her upper thighs, and took off down the street. Kendra leaned into me, her breasts pressing into my back. The roar of the engine, and the feeling of Kendra behind me, was exhilarating. Throughout the ride, all I could think about was her curvy body, her curly hair she'd pulled back into a ponytail for riding. Her lips were full and very kissable. And I'd fantasized about all the hot, dirty things I'd do to her once I got her into my bed again. By the time I pulled into the driveway at my house, I was starving but not for food.

I kept my hands to myself until we got into the house and then dragged Kendra into my arms, kissing her. "It's still early," I said, pulling back. "I think there's enough time for seconds on dinner and dessert."

Kendra snickered. "Greedy, greedy. Are you counting on me staying the night?"

I nodded. "Oh, I have been counting on it since before we

got into bed." I arched a brow. "Or would you rather preserve whatever illusions your grandma has about your romantic life?"

Kendra laughed, kissing the side of my neck. "I don't think she has any. As long as I'm not having sex under her roof, I'm sure it's a don't ask, don't tell situation."

I turned her face to mine and kissed her again. "Then let's heat up some of those leftovers and see where the night takes us."

"Now that's an idea I can get behind," Kendra commented, following me into the kitchen.

I started scooping up pasta and sauce and some leftover meat to feed us as I thought about Kendra's hesitation with the sheriff. "You know, if you wanted to give yourself a chance to heal and do the work without risking much in the way of flashbacks, Wampanoag isn't exactly Mayberry, but it also isn't Brooklyn or the Bronx."

"I know," Kendra said, shrugging as she took a plate from me and put it in the microwave to heat. "I'm thinking about it."

I looked at her for a second or two and then wrapped my arms around her, kissing the back of her neck. I would just have to give her a little time.

## 10

## KENDRA

"Okay," I said, stepping back to where the camera stood on its tripod. "Hold exactly like that." I grinned, still a little amazed at the way everything had fallen into place.

It had been just over a week since Grandma's birthday. I'd decided I would rather do the photo shoot for the firefighters' calendar as soon as possible. So a flurry of signing paperwork, checking out the equipment, and looking at previous editions—along with the current roster of both firefighters and animals to adopt—had all sped past. It had been ages since I'd done a shoot, but I fell right into the usual rhythm of setting up the shot, adjusting, and then shooting, letting my models change their positions a bit and kept going.

"I'm getting a cramp," one firefighter told me jokingly.

"Consider it a training exercise," I called back, stepping behind the camera and looking through the viewfinder. I took a quick breath, waited for exactly the right moment, and clicked the shutter. "Good! See if you can give me a little more smolder, though," I said to the two firefighters holding kittens.

"This isn't enough smolder?" one of them—Conrad—asked.

"Come on," I retorted. "You've got to get the ladies sweating." The two men laughed, shifting their positions so their muscles showed to the best advantage. They were almost as good as professional models—they'd done it a few times before. Only a few of the guys in the fire department were newbies, and I'd already taken care of their shots. I'd chosen a spot away from the station for about half of the photos, where I'd have a little more space to work with. Lukas was up the next day since the guys had to take turns being available to respond to emergencies while I was doing the shoots. I had to admit, I was looking forward to my photo shoot with Lukas.

I took a few more shots, getting Conrad and Finn to switch things up a bit each time, barely paying attention to the clock. I didn't have unlimited access to the firefighters during their sessions—the normal business of the day had to go on after all— but I had time enough to move around the groups, pairs, and solo shooting subjects. I got Conrad and Finn on their own, with different cats in their arms, cuddling them for the camera.

I finished up and sent the two firefighters on their way in order to set up for my next pair of men to take pictures of. "Tell everyone to take a shower before they come to see me," I told Conrad jokingly as he went off to enjoy the rest of his day.

"I'll tell them you will hose them down if they don't," Conrad joked back.

I'd done a shoot earlier in the day—while Conrad and Finn had waited their turn—featuring two other guys at the firehouse and two oversized puppies that would grow up into monsters. The only appropriate way to handle the muddiness of the fire-fighters and the energy of the dogs had been to hose everyone down and capture the results.

I put away the props for one setup and chatted with the handlers from the shelter, looking at the different animals they'd brought to include in the calendar. "I think it would be amazing to get big, buff Germaine with two tiny Chihuahuas," I said, looking into the kennel at Chatzi and Trinket—two little one-year-old Chihuahuas taken from an elderly woman who'd been hoarding pets—cuddled up to each other.

"Oh god—yeah, that would be perfect," Sherry, who was friends with my grandma, agreed. "And maybe Boscoe with that bean pole, Andrew?"

"Perfect," I said. Boscoe was an overweight Maine Coon, dark tabby colored, and he would look amazing in the arms of Lukas's fellow firefighter, Andrew—who was even taller than Lukas and had never grown out of his lanky phase.

I started getting my stuff together for the next set, and my cell rang. I took it out of my pocket, thinking it might be Lukas or Grandma—but the number that came up was the sheriff. I considered letting it roll over to voice mail, but my guilt nagged at me. If the sheriff was calling me, it was probably important. I tapped "accept."

"Hey, Kendra," Sheriff Baker said as soon as the line connected. "I know I don't have you in any official capacity and you still haven't decided what you want to do, career-wise, but I was wondering if I could ask you the favor of coming in and helping me out."

"What's going on, Sheriff?" I asked, stepping away from the ladies and the prospective pets, closer to my car. I could feel the twinge in my leg from standing and moving around so much, but I told myself I wouldn't have to stay on it for too much longer.

"Our B&E suspect has gone for it again," the sheriff informed me. "Last night. This time, he killed the victim, which is why we're only just now hearing about it. Could I have you come down to the station, look over the evidence we've collected?"

I thought about it hard. I didn't think I was ready for full-time police work again, but this was just one case. I wasn't sure I could deal with seeing a body—but if the prowler had graduated to murder after committing arson, we needed to catch him sooner rather than later, and the sheriff didn't have enough help on his force to get the job done.

"What kind of evidence do you have?" I questioned. That, at least, would give me an idea of whether I could handle it.

"We've got the body here," Sheriff Baker said. "I'm not expecting you to look at it—County ME is coming to pick it up and take it to the morgue. We're going over it for initial evidence. Medical examiner will give us anything we can't see with our own eyes. I've also got photos and some other details to look at."

I took a deep breath. *This is going to be tough.* But I hoped I could handle it.

"What's the clear cause of death?" If the ME was coming to take the body away, they only had the suspected cause to go by.

"Strangulation," Sheriff Baker replied. "Doc Soames determined that at the scene, so we could clear it. The victim, a male, had a female roommate—she didn't need to see all that, coming back from family shit."

I smiled to myself. That was the one big difference between small-town policing and New York City; the sheriff's consideration for the female roommate would never be on the list back in the city. There just wasn't time for it.

"I'm kind of in the middle of something," I told the sheriff. "Let me check on the progress of this project I'm on, and I'll get back to you in five to ten minutes."

"Sure thing," the sheriff answered. "I'm here all afternoon— the escalation of this criminal means I will need to field some calls, reassuring folks we're taking it seriously."

"Maybe you can get some extra resources from the state out of it," I suggested, smiling a bit despite how nervous the prospect of police work made me. "At least a bigger budget."

"Our very own special task force," the sheriff said, chuckling at the idea. "Turn Wampanoag into the biggest crime town in Vermont, outside of Burlington."

"Get that pretty face of yours on the news," I suggested.

Sheriff Baker laughed at that. "If there will be TV work, I'll get them to pay whatever it would take to lure you away from the NYPD to do it for me," he said. "You'd make a much better face of law enforcement in this town than I do." I laughed off the idea and hung up the phone, walking the rest of the way to my car to sit down.

I was undecided about what I wanted. On the one hand, I'd sworn an oath, and even though I'd done that in New York City, didn't it apply just as much anywhere else?

I had the skills and the experience Sheriff Baker needed to close this case, and if the only reason I didn't help him was concern about my mental state, what kind of cop was I?

My sergeant back at the precinct had called the day before, asking when I was going to take my evals to see if I could get back on duty.

If I wasn't ready, how much help would I be on a single case, even just as a consultant? I looked at my cell, pulling up Lukas's contact information, and started my text.

*Hi, Lukas. There's been another B&E, and this time, someone died...strangulation.*

*The sheriff wants me to come by and look at the full evidence for all the incidents, help him out.*

I tapped Send and looked around.

"Everything okay?" Sherry asked.

I nodded. "But I may have to reschedule," I told the women from the animal shelter. "Sheriff Baker wants my help on something."

"No worries," Sherry's partner, Jessica, said. "The critters enjoy being out and about, getting away from the shelter. We can bring them back another day."

My cell pinged. It was a message from Lukas.

*Are you sure you want to do it? Want me to come with?*

I sent a text back.

*I can handle it, I think. You're on call, right? I'll see what the sheriff has for me, what I can do for him.*

I started gathering up my gear to make sure it wouldn't be damaged by any random weather and loaded it into my SUV. By the time I was packed to go, I had another text from Lukas.

*Call me if you need me. If it's too much, you know? Otherwise, call me when you finish up.*

I smiled, promising him I would in a reply.

I called the sheriff, letting him know I was on my way in, then said goodbye to Sherry and Jessica.

$\cdot$ 11 $\cdot$

# LUKAS

As soon as Kendra told me she would work with the sheriff, I occupied myself as much as possible.

Being on call just meant hanging around, playing video games, eating at mealtimes with the rest of the crew—not that different from being on watch in the Army when it was a low-alert status. But I got to work doing side jobs, waiting to hear from Kendra. Not that I didn't think she could handle it, but I wanted to be ready to get to her if there was an issue.

While I worked, I thought about the past week, how fast things had gone between Kendra and me. Some of it was definitely because we'd known each other so well as kids. But there was something about how quickly we'd gone from coffee to practically being a couple that set off alarm bells in my head.

I'd grown up watching the dynamic between Mom and the man that I called my sperm donor. The way he'd treated her like shit, being verbally abusive, controlling her, making her life a living hell. As I cleaned a pair of spare boots to get them ready for the next muster, I wondered how his verbal abuse started.

My cell rang as I put away my boots, and I almost dropped it trying to pick it up fast. It was Kendra. "Hey, how are you?" I probed as soon as the line connected.

Kendra's breath hitched over the line. My chest tightened with worry.

"I need help," she whispered. "I'm not in danger, but..."

"What happened?"

Kendra sighed. "Toward the end of my meeting with the sheriff, a bunch of men did drills with their weapons. I could hold it together to finish up with Baker, but I'm not sure I'm okay to drive."

I had my keys in my hand before Kendra even finished her sentence. "I'll be right there. The sheriff's office is only two blocks away." I couldn't stay on the phone with her and ride my bike, so I ended the call, walking out of the building, and headed straight for my cycle. Nobody was likely to miss me for the ten or fifteen minutes it would take to check on Kendra and bring her back. I doubted there would be two fires at once in that time.

When I arrived, Kendra was in a corner of the parking lot, still shivering in her SUV. Right away, I knew there would not be a good way to get her to ride with me on my bike—she was too shaky and out of it. I took her keys from her, pulling her into my arms and holding her tightly. On instinct, I rubbed her back and kissed the top of her head, feeling her curly hair against my face.

I held her for a few minutes until she stopped trembling so hard. Pulling back, I asked, "I will drive you to the station, okay?"

Kendra frowned. "You're just going to leave the bike here?"

I shrugged. "It's not that far. I can get someone to drop me off on the way home or something. Worst-case scenario, I can walk it at the end of shift."

Kendra still looked doubtful. "I don't want to put you out. Maybe..."

I put my finger on her lips, stopping her from saying another word. "Kendra, get in the passenger side, and let me take you to the station to chill for a bit." I stared into her beautiful hazel eyes until she nodded her agreement.

Hurrying over to the passenger side, I helped Kendra inside before climbing into the driver's seat, turning on the vehicle, and taking off toward the firehouse. A few blocks later, we arrived, and I led Kendra away from where the rest of the guys were having a *Fortnite* tournament in the rec area.

I hugged her again. "Do you want something to eat? Drink?"

Kendra shook her head, taking a few deep breaths. "I think the worst part of it is over. It was just..." Her eyes darted away then back to me. "Hearing the noise. And then it was being so fucking pissed at myself for still losing my shit so easily."

"Kendra, take it easy on yourself. It takes time to get through these kinds of things. And you can't keep trying to be the person you were before it happened—otherwise, you're just going to keep getting pissed at yourself." I kissed her lightly on the lips and smiled.

"I know," Kendra said, her face starting to look a little less tense. "Thank you for being there."

"Whatever you need from me, I'll be there for you, baby," I replied huskily, and I meant it. Whenever she needed me, regardless of whether she stayed in town, I'd be there for her.

She laced her fingers together behind my neck. "You know, I seem to recall a promise that you made. Something about if I stayed in town and if I had flashbacks."

I laughed. I could tell she was joking—but I couldn't deny that just having her in my arms, feeling her body against mine, and seeing her start to look better had stirred something primal in me.

"There are beds in the on-call room," I pointed out, letting my hands drop to her waist and giving her a careful squeeze. "And the guys are loud enough on *Fortnite* that we could make all kinds of noise, and nobody would even notice."

Kendra laughed and gave me a playful shove against my shoulder. "You just want everyone to know for sure you're sleeping with me."

"Well, that would be a bonus," I joked. "You're the hottest

woman in town." Plus, I was a territorial bastard. I'd seen the looks Kendra got from most of the men at the firehouse and in town. I wanted to stake my claim on the most beautiful, smartest, toughest woman around.

Kendra rolled her eyes. "You are a perv."

I cupped her ass. "Only with you."

The alarm went off, and I released my hold on her butt and pinned her to my side.

"Fire! 2254 West Elmbrook!" The chief shouted over the PA. The men on duty rushed past to get geared up and on the truck, and I held on to Kendra, worried the emergency might trigger her again. Instead, she just wrapped her arm around my waist. Once the fury of a bunch of men rushing out subsided, she looked up into my face and said, "Wow! That was interesting."

"More than half the crew left," I pointed out. "We could just go lie down and cuddle for a bit."

"You really want me in bed, huh?" Kendra asked, giving me that playful, defiant look that only made me hornier.

I reached down and cupped her ass. "Desperately." Clutching her hand, I led her back through the station to the on-call rooms. By the time I got the door closed and locked behind us, I was more than ready to pin Kendra against it and kiss her harder, letting my hands move over her tight, curvy body. I tugged her T-shirt free of her jeans and touched the impossibly soft, hot skin underneath.

"You better not get too loud," Kendra murmured as I cupped her full breasts in my hands through her bra.

"Me? Better worry about yourself," I countered before kissing her again. We stayed like that for a few minutes, kissing and stroking each other until I couldn't take it anymore. I pulled Kendra away from the door and started stripping her down, hauling her shirt over her head and tossing it aside. I buried my face against her chest, nuzzling her breasts and reaching around to her back to unhook her bra. She got to work on my jeans, getting the fly open and starting to tug them down before my shirt was even off.

Lifting her up, I carried her over to one of the bottom bunks, gently dropping and pinning her to the bed. It took only seconds for me to get her naked, then I stripped.

"You're in a hurry," Kendra said, breathless and with that tone in her voice that told me it definitely turned her on.

"Another call could come in at any minute," I pointed out. "And I promised to get you off." Kendra laughed, and I made my way down from her lips to her chest, bringing each of her dark nipples up to my mouth to suck and lick. She moaned. I'd learned fast just what got Kendra hot. I worked the firm little nubs with my mouth for what felt like ages, even as my cock grew harder. Reaching between her legs, I felt how wet she was and moved from her chest to her stomach, breathing in the tantalizing scent of her skin and pussy.

I buried my face against her pussy, licking and sucking. Sliding my tongue up and down along her folds, tasting her as thoroughly as possible. I stroked my tongue over her clit, knowing exactly what she liked. I gently sucked the little bead of nerves between my lips, swirling the tip of my tongue around it in wide circles to get her used to the sensation and then zeroing in on it.

Kendra's hips bucked, and I pinned them down, careful to avoid doing anything that would hurt her injured leg. I worked Kendra hot and heavy, teasing her just enough to get her more turned on, feeling the changes in her as she got closer and closer to getting off. She moaned, and then I looked up when I heard a more unusual sound and saw that she was covering her mouth with one of her hands—the other tangled in my hair—to keep from being too loud. I almost broke away, laughing, but I hadn't been lying when I'd said a call could come in at any moment. Time was absolutely of the essence.

I decided not to tease her too hard, to do what I knew would get Kendra off instead of waiting my turn. I sucked harder on her womanhood, flicking my tongue against the little bead between my lips, and Kendra's hand tightened in my hair, almost pulling it from the scalp. I moaned against her skin, working her as hard as I could, feeling the tension in her hitting the high point. I knew the second she came, her fluids starting to gush on my tongue as her legs tightened around me, as her whole body shook for just a few seconds in between moments of tensing up. Kendra moaned long and low, and even her hand didn't muffle the noise—at least, not to me.

I kept her coming for as long as I could stand and then pulled back, not even giving her a chance to come down from the climax. I got a condom out of a drawer in the table next to the bunk, sheathed my cock, then covered her body with mine again. "Next time," I told her breathlessly between kisses. "Next time, I'm making you ride me."

"With my leg? That'd last all of a minute," Kendra told me.

I laughed. "Excuses." I didn't have any patience to make it last—my balls were aching and, besides, I wasn't about to answer a call with my dick hard. I pounded into Kendra's pussy hard and fast, kissing her neck and then up to her lips as I pulled out and slammed back in again. I set a pace that was just short of brutal, hauling Kendra's legs up by the knees and wrapping them around my waist to get a better angle. She felt good, tight, hot, and built just for me. Her muscles flexed around me, tightening in little post-orgasmic spasms, and that just fueled me to go faster, to take her harder. Kendra had no complaints, pushing her hips up to meet mine, kissing me hungrily as we moved together sensually.

It didn't take me long to feel my balls starting to tighten, to feel that ache in my groin hitting the point where there was only one way to get rid of it. I held on to Kendra as tightly as I could and pounded into her a few more times, moaning as the tension broke. I came hard, going only a little while longer, and I realized that Kendra had reached her second climax while I was on my first, that she was gripping me with all her strength as we both finished.

"God, I needed that," I said, kissing her lightly on the lips.

"Who you telling. Damn, that was better than a Xanax," Kendra told me.

I laughed, rolling off her just long enough to dispose of the used condom in the bin. Whoever tossed out the bio-waste would have questions, but I could guarantee he wouldn't ask anyone why there was a used condom in among the bloody bandages and gauze from treating different work-related wounds. I climbed back onto the bed at her side, pulling her close and loving the feeling of her body against mine.

"I kind of doubt doctors can prescribe orgasms," I pointed out.

Kendra grinned at me, looking so beautiful, so sweet in the crook of my arm. "They used to, actually," she said. "And I guess PTSD would count as 'hysteria,' so you getting me off is just good medicine."

I laughed and cupped one of her breasts in my hand, enjoying the heavy, warm feeling of it. Before I could get up the energy to go for round two, though, the alarm blared again, and I was on my feet, out of the bed, and pulling on my clothes in an instant. Kendra got up almost as quickly, pulling on her clothes.

"Do you want to hang out here?" I asked her as the chief announced the fire location. It wasn't too far away. "I probably won't be more than two hours, tops."

"No. I've got to head home," Kendra said. "Grandma doesn't know about me helping the sheriff, and she's expecting me for dinner."

"I'll text you once I'm done," I promised, kissing her again once we were both fully dressed.

"And tomorrow, we have the photo shoot," Kendra said. "Maybe we can compare sex in an SUV to the on-call beds."

I chuckled and unlocked the door before anyone could come

looking for me. "I'd be down with that experiment," I said before kissing her hard and fast.

"I bet you would," she chirped before we parted ways, with Kendra headed out to the parking lot to get in her SUV, and me heading for the second truck where we stowed the gear to take care of the fire.

❧  12  ❧

## KENDRA

Grandma set down my plate in front of me before taking her spot at the table. Dinner was one of her classics—Salisbury steak with roasted potatoes, carrots, and green beans. It brought me back to being a teenager, living with her, telling her all about my day at school, back when my problems were much smaller.

Grandma gave me a knowing look before forking a piece of carrot. "So, you've been busy for someone who's supposed to be resting."

I grinned because she was right. "Are you sure you don't just resent that I haven't weeded the garden beds yet?" I asked, cutting into my meat. I'd had many Salisbury steaks in my life, from school cafeteria versions to a diner on Brook Avenue that claimed to make it the best in the city—but none of them were as good as Grandma's.

"That's part of it," Grandma confessed. "But I'm also worried about you. You're supposed to be recuperating, not rushing off every day to do something else."

I took a bite of food, chewing thoughtfully before swallowing. "Well, I finished the photo shoot the other day, and tomorrow I'll have the proofs printed for the chief. That's one project done." I'd been back in town for two weeks, and it was almost as if I'd never left. Somehow—probably mostly because of Grandma and her friends talking me up—everyone knew everything about me, and I was anxious at merely the thought of going back to the constant rush of the city. But I could feel it pulling me, reaching for me like a comfortable pair of sweat pants.

"And you're working with the sheriff," Grandma observed. "How do you feel about that?" She grabbed her glass of water, sipping.

I picked at a carrot, suddenly not feeling so hungry. "I'm not sure," I admitted. "He wants me to join the force officially, especially since the press is heating up on the serial break-ins."

"Are you ready to handle that pressure?" Grandma asked, taking a bite of potato.

"That kind of thing doesn't bother me," I stated. "But there's another issue." I bit my bottom lip, twirling my fork.

"Lukas?" Grandma asked.

"Partly him," I sighed. "But mostly, they want me back down in the city. Sarge has called twice to ask when I think I'll be ready for the evals."

"Are you surprised?" She arched a brow. "You've got to be one of the best people he has."

I laughed. "You'd think so, based on how he's working me," I told her. "And obviously, my record was good."

"Good?" Grandma snorted. "I've looked at your record on that devil machine they call a personal computing device. Your record is better than almost everyone else from your precinct."

"So, you've been checking up on me that hard?" I asked. If Grandma had gotten out the computer and used it, she must have been interested.

"Well, you never tell me anything, and I needed to keep everyone up-to-date on my beautiful granddaughter's career," Grandma said. "If I didn't, Mabel might have all the good stories —what with that great-nephew of hers running some fancy club in LA."

"My record is good," I muttered, absently spearing two green beans on my fork. "But I'm not sure I want to go back to New York. I'm not even sure I want to be a cop anymore." I hadn't told Grandma about the bigger issue. Because of my leg, they'd keep me on desk duty for as long as it took to heal—that would be no problem. But the psychological issue of my PTSD was a whole other clusterfuck.

"And you're working through the whole PTSD thing," Grandma countered.

I looked up, surprised. "You know?"

Grandma shrugged. "Your grandfather was in a war. He never said much about it, but he had friends who would get drunk and get—I don't know—twitchy. Any little thing might set them off. They used to call it 'shell shock.'"

"But Granddaddy didn't have it?"

Grandma shrugged again. "He might have, he might not have. I'm just saying, I can see when someone is working through something—especially when that someone is the girl I helped raise."

She was right. Grandma knew me well. "Lukas's been helping me with it," I volunteered. "In different ways. He knows some guys with PTSD."

"I understand he's done a lot of work along those lines, though probably not as intensely as he has with you," Grandma said, smiling a little.

"It's just..." I began.

"It's just you reconnecting with a boy you might have had something with, if things had gone differently," Grandma said, interrupting me. "And now, because you're afraid it's got some potential, you want to run."

"No, I don't want to run," I protested. At least, I didn't think so.

"Kendra, you're afraid," Grandma said with sharp eyes. "Terrified of not getting better. Scared of what it would be like if you changed because of getting injured. And you're petrified that it means you're too broken for Lukas. But listen here, baby girl, Lukas cut his teeth on issues harder than this."

"So, what do you think I should do?" Because honestly, this conundrum was shit I'd never dealt with before.

Grandma looked at me for a long moment, then brought a forkful of potatoes and meat to her mouth, chewing and swallowing with her usual perfect manners before she answered me. "You're grown, so I can't tell you what you should do. But I can tell you it would be a lot easier to recover from something like what you went through if you're in a quiet, peaceful place. When you're not chasing down drug dealers every week or investigating murders all the time. Wampanoag might be this side of boring, but you could do well here. And I think if I had a chance like what you've got with Lukas, I'd take it in a heartbeat."

I thought about that for a few minutes as I ate my food, weighing what she said against what I had spent so much of the past two weeks thinking about. "I agree about Wampanoag being a place where I'd be able to find some peace and solace, but—" I paused "—as far as Lukas and me, I don't even know if he wants to be serious. This could just be a fling for him." Deep down, I was leaning toward trying to see if he and I could make what we had more than just fucking. But turning my back on my job in New York... That bothered me.

Grandma took a sip from her glass of water. "It might be," she said, her voice skeptical. "But I don't believe flings are his thing, or he already would have slept with half the town. From what I've heard and seen, all the single women and some not-so-unattached females in town have propositioned him. He's turned them all down. But a man that handsome, not settling down... people will talk. Hell, some folks have even started speculating he's gay."

I nearly choked on a piece of meat before finally clearing my throat. "Lukas, gay?" I chuckled. "Believe me, he's definitely not gay."

Grandma grinned. "I'm glad you have firsthand knowledge of

that. And talk to him about you thinking about staying here and if he's interested in more than rolling around in the hay."

I snickered at her "rolling around in the hay" phrase but took her advice to heart.

She continued, "And another thing." She jabbed a finger at me. "Don't let your sergeant rush you into a decision, no matter what you do."

"I won't," I mumbled, eating a little more of her delicious steak. "One day, you will need to give me your secrets for this." I pointed my fork at the steak on my plate. "You will not be around forever, and nobody else makes it like you."

"Grind your own grass-fed meat and use a Lipton onion soup packet in the gravy," Grandma said with a grin. "That's all it is, baby girl."

I laughed. "No, it's not. I saw you sneaking tablespoons of your homemade special seasoning into the meat before you cooked it."

Her eyes widened. "You saw that?"

"I did. I'm a detective." I pointed my fork at her. "I see everything."

"You're too smart for your own good." She rolled her eyes. "Now, eat your food and be quiet."

We started eating again, and a comfortable silence blanketed us. It was then that it really hit me how much I missed simple things like eating dinner with her. She was my world and my only family, and I didn't know how much more time I had with her before she was no longer here. *Why the hell did I stay away from her for so long?*

"I love you, Grandma," I blurted out.

Grandma froze, her fork midway to her mouth. "I love you too, Kendra. More than you'll ever know." She winked at me before continuing to eat.

I blinked back tears of emotion. I'd sacrificed so much for the sake of my career and making detective and had very little to show for my efforts, all because I'd made a conscious decision that my job came first. There was nothing back in New York but my job. I had no boyfriend or lover waiting for me to return and no girlfriends missing our weekly "Girls' Night Out" and chomping at the bit for me to come back. Yes, my job as a detective was important. *But wasn't having a life filled with happiness, family, love, good health, and friendship more vital?*

My mind whirled with all the life-changing decisions I'd have to make; the most important determination was whether to stay here or go back to New York to my old job and life.

It was ironic how, in just a few weeks back in town, I'd started thinking about the possibility of a new life that included seeing Grandma every day, a less risky, more laid-back job working with the sheriff, and just maybe, something more permanent with Lukas.

But it scared me to walk away from the career I'd built in New York and to try something different.

## 13

## LUKAS

I spotted Kendra looking beautiful as usual as she sat at the table she'd taken at McDuffy's—an old-school diner in town where we'd eaten plenty of meals on Friday or Saturday nights as kids. It smelled like it always had—grease, burgers, and bacon, with a splash of fresh orange juice cutting through it. And as I stepped around the tables to get to the one Kendra had chosen next to a window, I almost felt as if I'd gone back in time.

I leaned down, giving her a quick kiss before sitting. "This was a great idea. I don't think I've been here in months."

"I figured it would be a good change-up from you cooking for me," Kendra stated.

I chuckled. "But I love cooking for you."

"I adore you for it." She sent me an air kiss.

"This place has one downside. My bedroom isn't only a few steps away," I pointed out.

"That's the truth," she agreed with a saucy smile.

A waitress, Barb, came to the table, and we both ordered our usual choices from back in the old days, the cheeseburger "Royale" for me, which had a fried egg on it, with cheese fries, and a meatloaf melt for Kendra, with zesty fries for her side. We got beers and settled in to wait for our food to come up.

"So, did you sleep in like you were planning?" Kendra asked me.

I'd been too exhausted after a few emergencies at the end of my shift to invite her over the night before. But we'd texted back and forth, planning to meet up since it was my day off.

"I got a good nine hours," I told her, stretching at the memory of waking up fully rested. Refreshed in a way I hadn't been in years—and that, I could confidently say, was almost definitely to do with Kendra coming back into my life and our spending quality time together and getting to know each other again. It was not just on a physical level, but I would never complain about our fantastic sexual chemistry, which was a hell of a bonus. I beamed at her. "Maybe we should go back to my place after this so I can show you all the wicked things I can do to your sexy body when I'm fully charged." I waggled my eyebrows.

"Maybe." Her eyes shifted away then back to me.

I looked at her a little more intently. Years of living with my father, with his outbursts, had trained my brain to recognize the slightest difference in someone I was close to. I'd gone through the therapy—it was part of encouraging my buddies from the Army to get help for their problems. And, in fact, I'd had a therapist tell me he was sure that part of how I'd come through my deployments without getting PTSD was because all the trauma of my childhood had more or less inoculated me to it. But it had left me with the hypervigilance, if not the other symptoms.

"What's up?" I asked. Barb brought our drinks to the table, so Kendra couldn't answer right away. We took sips of our beers, and I kept waiting for her to tell me what was going on.

She sighed heavily. "My sergeant is trying to push hard for me to come back."

She'd mentioned him calling once or twice, but judging by the unusual tension displayed on her face, there was more to it.

I leaned forward. "How is he pushing?" I asked, trying to keep my tone as neutral as possible. "And are you saying that you want to go?" *She isn't just going to run away to NYC, is she? Without giving us a chance at more?*

"I've got a great record," Kendra revealed. "He wants me to go for the evaluation next week, then a stint on desk duty depending how the psych part goes."

I clenched my fingers around the beer bottle. "So, you want to go back next week?" I demanded.

"I don't know if I want to go back at all," Kendra protested. "But honestly, I'm not sure if agreeing to take the job here is the right thing for me."

"So why does it matter if your sergeant is pressuring you?" I countered. "Can't you tell him to back off?"

"Can we enjoy our meal before we get into an argument about this?" Kendra picked at the tablecloth and then sipped her beer.

I took a deep breath and made myself calm down. "I'm just trying to understand."

Barb brought our food to the table. The service at McDuffy's was always quick.

"Let's enjoy our meal," Kendra suggested. "Then we can discuss what I will do."

"Fine," I replied.

I took a bite of my burger, making myself focus on the taste of it—fatty, meaty, and delicious. I watched as Kendra started in on her meatloaf sandwich.

Kendra avoided eye contact with me as she ate, and the silence between us stretched. What should have been an enjoyable meal with the woman I adored was turning into a nightmare.

"Okay," Kendra said finally, setting her food partly aside. "Can you let me explain everything to you before you react?"

"Yes. I'll do that," I promised, putting down my burger and eating one of my fries.

"The long and short of it is that I don't know what I want to do," Kendra said. "I feel like I owe a lot to the NYPD."

"And?" I said.

Kendra's eyes narrowed.

I shrugged. "I'm not reacting. I'm just prompting."

She carried on, "I want to end things in New York on a high note."

"So, you're going back." Anger flared at the thought of losing Kendra, but I refused to rant and rave like I'd always seen my father do when shit didn't go his way. I'd fought for years against the idea that something destined me to be like him, that I had anything in common with that man at all, apart from the bad luck to have some of his genes and to have spent my childhood around the asshole.

"I have to," she snapped.

I snorted. "You mean, you want to." I took a sip of beer.

"You don't under—"

I cut her off. "And what about us?" I arched a brow. "Are we going to do that whole long-distance relationship thing?"

Her shoulders sagged. "Lukas, long-distance relationships never work."

"Right." I narrowed my eyes. "So, just like that, we're done."

"Lukas..."

"Kendra, you mean the world to me." My voice was husky. "And I'm willing to fight tooth and nail to make our relationship work." Reaching over, I grabbed her hand, weaving my fingers through hers. "You know why?"

Tears glistened in her eyes. "No," she rasped.

"Because I can see forever with you, Kendra Powell."

"Fuck. Lukas, don't make this hard for me." She bit her bottom lip.

I was sure I was falling in love. Not that I had any examples of a loving, healthy relationship—my parents' marriage had been toxic and volatile. All I had were my gut feelings that Kendra was a woman I could love and protect for the rest of my life. But thinking about such a commitment was too soon for me and for her.

"You are my woman. And before you walked back into my life, I didn't give a shit about having a woman in my life. In fact, I wanted to spend my life alone." The last part sounded selfish as fuck, but it was the truth. "You're the first woman I've ever wanted more with. But my feelings can't be one-sided. Want me too." I pulled my hands away from hers.

"I do, Lukas. I'm just not strong enough to walk away from what I know to walk into the unknown with you."

"Okay," I said flatly.

"Okay?" She frowned. "That's all you have to say?"

"Yes." My heart hammered. "I won't force you to want us. You either do or you don't." Each word was like a stab to the gut. "I told you how I feel..." And she hadn't reciprocated, which was very telling. It was fucking with my head that I'd misread our whole relationship, that I thought we were actually building a solid relationship that went beyond just fantastic sex. "And what I want, which is you." I paused. "I want us, but you don't. And if you're expecting me to fly into some asshole rage about it. I'm not that kind of man, Kendra. I'm not like my father, who forced my mother to give up her dreams just to be with him and cater to his ego."

Kendra replied immediately, "You don't understand how scary this is for me to decide about my career based on our relationship. I've spent years focused on my career and making detective, and then some asswipe comes along and shoots me, taking away what I've worked so hard for. I can't even fucking hear firecrackers without losing my shit. And now you expect me to give up my life in New York too?"

"I don't expect shit, Kendra. You've made your decision, and I will not argue about it." My cell buzzed. *Shit. It's the chief.* "It's a text from the fire station. There's a big fire at the plant. I need to go in."

"Duty calls." She sighed heavily. "We'll talk later."

I signaled for Barb, our waitress, who came over quickly. "Check, please," I demanded.

"Be right back," she chirped before hustling away. She was back in a jiffy, giving me the check.

I stared at Kendra while peeling out enough cash to cover the amount of our meal plus tip. "I don't enjoy leaving like this." It bothered the hell out of me that I'd had to leave before we'd finished our discussion. Her deciding to leave was still fucking with my head, but it was her decision whether I liked it or not.

"I understand." Kendra looked at me. The disappointment on her face was almost worse than anger.

I scooted my chair closer, leaning in. I kissed her slow and easy like we had all the time in the world. But we didn't. Kendra was leaving town, and I couldn't stop her. Breaking off our kiss, I stood, walking away from her...forever.

❧ 14 ❧

# KENDRA

"What is *Pride and Prejudice?*" the *Jeopardy* contestant on the TV asked. I snorted.

"It's *Sense and Sensibility*," I told Grandma.

I sipped a glass of water Grandma had insisted I needed. I had gotten out of the habit of staying hydrated while I was working, but Grandma had brought it all back with her insistence on glasses of water several times a day. "Good for the kidneys, good for the liver, good for the spleen, and great for the skin," she always said.

"I'm sorry," Alex Trebek told the contestant. "The correct answer was *Sense and Sensibility*."

"You should go on the show," Grandma said, giving me a proud look. Even before I'd lived with her when I was young, she'd encouraged me to read as much as possible. And when I'd moved to her place after Mom had died, she'd insisted on my reading fifty books a year, one for almost every week. I got the occasional pass on longer books and sometimes made up for lost time with short ones, but on average, I made it through. I was the best-read detective in my precinct, and even after college, I still read at least twenty books a year.

"I'd bomb in that Art History category," I pointed out.

"Books, I know. History, I'm good at. Psych and Criminology, I'm great. But I've got big gaps."

"Just make some of your books more well rounded," Grandma suggested.

I smiled, shifting in the chair I'd taken. It was a ritual from my childhood, watching *Jeopardy* with Grandma either during or after dinner, talking about the categories and the contestants. But I felt off tonight, despite the familiarity. I was leaving in a few days, and frankly, I'd miss her something fierce once gone.

When I'd told Grandma I was going back to New York, she just said, "Baby girl, why would you want to walk away from a new beginning just to go back to a past you know you don't want?" Deep down in my heart, I knew she was right. But the mere thought of walking away from a career I'd fought for with lots of blood, sweat, and tears broke me out in a cold sweat.

And then there was Lukas.

A wave of sadness washed over me when I remembered the hurt and anger in his eyes the night I told him I was going back to my job.

I couldn't pinpoint when our relationship had moved from just sex to more, but it had. I was falling in love with him, and that new dynamic worried me.

*What if I stayed, and our relationship went south?*
*Could we go back to friendship?*
*No. We couldn't.*

I knew from the moment we'd first had sex that we couldn't go back to being just friends. What Lukas and I had was too complex, too passionate, and too deep. We had an all-in or all-out kind of relationship, which was why it both irked and hurt me that he'd kept his distance since our diner debacle. He'd only sent me a text saying, "I'm here for you if you need me. But I'm giving you space."

I nibbled my bottom lip, feeling like at any moment I would break out into a hot, ugly cry. I knew what he was really doing was pulling away from me, from us. But I couldn't blame him. At the diner, he hadn't pulled any punches when he'd told me how he'd felt about me and what he wanted—me. Instead of telling him what I'd suspected for a long time, that I was falling in love with him, I sat there, struggling to sort through my overwhelming feelings and putting them into words that made sense.

*Stop lying, Kendra. You didn't tell him how you felt because you were too fucking scared to reveal your feelings.* It had been a big mistake not to at least tell him what I was starting to feel.

But the real kick to my gut was the kiss he gave me that felt like goodbye before walking away from me and out of the diner.

"You okay, baby girl?" Grandma asked, cutting through my thoughts. "You've gone quiet over there."

"Yeah. Just tired," I told her. It was the only lie I could get away with around her, and I wasn't sure I even convinced her—just that it was one of few kinds of lie she would play along with for me. "I think I will turn in early."

"Okay, see you in the morning," Grandma replied.

I finished my glass of water and went up to my room, grabbing the hand towel that I used for drying my face, and walked into the bathroom. I started washing my face with my favorite cleansing oil, trying to compose my mind into less stressful thoughts before I went to bed. I failed and shut off the water, disgusted with myself. I patted my face dry and reached for my bottle of argan oil, but just as I got the bottle open, I heard something.

At first, I didn't even know what it was I heard, but it sent the hairs on the back of my neck straight up before it even filtered through my brain. Years of training and experience rose to the surface, and I set the bottle down as quietly as possible, silently creeping out of the bathroom and toward the living room.

Grandma shouted at the same time I heard a loud crashing, glass-shattering noise. Instead of padding out, I ran the last few feet into the living room with so much adrenaline coursing through me, I forgot all about my injured leg.

My brain went on to autopilot when I saw some man in dirty, ripped clothes lunging for Grandma.

"Get down!" I shouted at him in the tone I'd used countless times as a police officer.

Instead, the man grabbed Grandma with one hand, and the other brandished a knife he jabbed in the air erratically, using it to keep me away.

I did a quick assessment of the situation, and despite her life-and-death situation, Grandma was calm. *Smart, Grandma.* I didn't need her making any sudden movements because from the glassy haze of the man's eyes and his twitchy body, he was high on something and would hurt her.

"Put the knife down, and let her go," I ordered, moving within striking distance.

I scanned the living room and didn't see that the intruder had anything to cart away valuables with. If he'd intended on doing that, he likely would have gone for a less conspicuous entry. Either he was the worst burglar of all time, or he was the prowler Sheriff Baker and I had been tracking. But he wasn't there to steal from us.

The man glared at me from behind Grandma. He wasn't even using his weapon as a threat against Grandma.

"If you're looking for prescription drugs," I said calmly, "We don't have any."

"What the fuck are you talking about?" His voice cracked. His grip slipped away from Grandma's body.

"Move, Grandma," I barked while I attacked, striking him hard in the knees. Grandma dashed to the left and safety. The intruder instinctively put his arms out defensively as he fell, bracing for floor impact, releasing the knife, and it clattered to the floor.

Kicking his weapon out of reach, I checked Grandma over quickly. "You okay?"

"I'm fine, baby," Grandma said as we watched the man scramble unsteadily to his feet. "Get the bastard."

I leaped forward to grab him, and I yelped in pain when the muscles in my leg rebelled against my sudden movement. I cursed under my breath as the guy made a mad dash through the house and into the kitchen. There was a door in the kitchen that led out into the backyard, and I wondered how long he'd spent casing Grandma's place, thinking about his contingencies.

Pushing away the pain in my leg, I chased the prowler through the house and into the kitchen, intent on tackling him down.

I made it into the kitchen just as the asshole turned on the gas at the stove full blast, and he produced some kind of tiny bulb of liquid from a pocket on his dark cargo pants. He threw it at the stove, and the fire jumped out from the combination of leaking gas and accelerant and whatever else he'd included.

"You son of a bitch," I growled, rushing for him anyway. The fire was a problem, but I would take care of that in a second. First, I was taking down the asshole who'd threatened Grandma.

I moved on instinct. Running toward him like a freight train, I banged him into the kitchen wall before letting loose a flurry of kicks and punches that I'd learned from my many practice sessions with an ex-MMA fighter I'd worked out with in New York. The intruder wasn't much of a fighter because he didn't react offensively by attacking me. Instead, he grunted and begged for his life. But I wasn't having any of that shit. He'd broken in to my house, and I had the right to defend myself. I grabbed him, knocking his head against the wall several times before his eyes rolled to the back of his head. I sidestepped when his body fell to the floor, unconscious.

The heat of the fire was raging out of control. "Fuck." The kitchen was on fire, and it was not something I could handle on my own. I had to get out. I stared at the unconscious man. I wouldn't be able to handle it if I let him burn to death, especially not without facing justice for his crimes. After opening the door in the kitchen that led out into the backyard, I walked back to the intruder, yanking him across the floor by the leg. The muscles in my injured leg were protesting from the strain, but I finally made it out into the yard with the asshole intruder.

Hearing a sound of feet behind me, I turned to see Grandma and her neighbor Mr. Seibert heading toward me.

I smiled with relief that she'd made it out safely, but I'd know she would.

"I called 9-1-1," Grandma said to me.

"Who the hell is that?" Mr. Seibert asked, gesturing to the unconscious man on the grass.

"I'm guessing the guy who's been terrorizing the town," I said, finally letting the enormity of the situation catch up with me.

"Good job," Mr. Seibert said, nodding his approval.

* * *

I was half dressed and my leg was killing me, but I leaned against my SUV, proud of myself. I'd subdued and apprehended a serial burglar and murderer.

The fire truck roared up to the house, and Lukas was the first man off it. He glanced anxiously around and spotted me as the rest of the men on the crew got to work on setting up the hose to put out the blaze.

Lukas stormed over to me, fully geared up. "You're okay?" he asked, reaching up to cup my cheek.

I nodded. "Yes. But my leg is killing me," I said. "Don't worry about me. Go see if you can't salvage some of Grandma's kitchen, will you?"

"Yes, ma'am," Lukas replied with a smile. He hurried off to the house with the rest of the firefighters.

The police arrived hot on the heels of the fire truck, and Sheriff Baker nearly leaped out of his car, hurrying to where I stood with Grandma and Mr. Seibert, the prowler still tied up on the ground nearby. "Whoa!" the sheriff exclaimed, taking in the sight of the man bound on the grass.

"Based on how he acted," I said, "I think we have our man, Sheriff."

"What makes you so sure?" Sheriff Baker asked.

I kicked the prowler's foot and pointed out a key feature on the sole of one shoe—nails, hammered in, that had created the same mark we'd seen at all the crime scenes.

"If nothing else," I said, once the sheriff had taken in that fact in, "he's definitely guilty of attempted murder, arson, and breaking and entering for tonight." One of the sheriff's deputies came up, and Baker filled the man in.

"Good catch, Powell," Sheriff Baker said. "It sounds like the way you handled yourself was a credit to your training."

"She sure as hell did," Grandma agreed.

"You know, Sheriff Baker," I said, looking over as the firefighters began to come out of Grandma's house. There hadn't been enough time for the fire to spread to the rest of the house. "I've given it a lot of thought, and I believe I'd like to accept your offer to transfer here."

"I'd love to have you," Baker said. "And after the news gets a load of this, I can safely say that the town would ride me out on a rail if I didn't insist on you bringing your skills here."

"Why, thank you," I replied with a grin. Given everything I'd just been through, all the thoughts that had been swirling in my brain had crystallized. I was ready for a new start, and this town was everything I needed. Whether or not things worked out with Lukas, I could have a future in Wampanoag. And it would do me more good handling the small-town crimes than it had working in the high-stress, fast-paced world of the NYPD.

I broke out laughing when Lukas came out of the house with Grandma's favorite Bundt pan in his hands—she'd gotten it from her mother when she was barely out of her teens. He handed it to Grandma before tossing aside his helmet, rushing over to me, and grabbing me around the waist.

"You mean the world to me, Kendra," Lukas said, staring into my eyes. "I can't lose you."

Reaching up, I cupped his cheek. "Well, then it's a good thing I promised the sheriff I would stay."

Lukas looked at me in disbelief for a few moments and then grinned. "Really?" he asked.

I nodded. "Yes," I told him. "My job in New York was great, but as a wise woman—" my gaze flicked over to Grandma, who gave me a thumbs-up "—pointed out, why would I want to walk away from a new beginning just to go back to a past I know I don't want anymore?"

"Sounds like a very intelligent woman," he murmured while running his hands across my back.

"Very," I answered.

"So, you and me?" he asked, nibbling my bottom lip.

"Definitely a go, firefighter," I answered before swiping my tongue over his lips. "You're my man, and I'm not letting you go without a fight."

"About time, woman," he answered before he slid his hand to my jaw. He tilted his head before he settled his lips across my mouth. My breath caught. He slid his tongue between my teeth. The kiss was long and deep—the stamp of his possession—and I loved it.

❧ 15 ❧

# KENDRA

**Two years later...**

Lukas and I stepped out of the country club and onto the lawn to the sounds of loud cheering and clapping. Lukas squeezed my hand, prompting me to look up at him. "Are you okay?" he asked. I knew he was worried about my reaction to the noise. I was still in treatment for PTSD ever since I'd resigned from the NYPD and joined the Sheriff's Department in Wampanoag.

"I'm fine," I assured him as we made our way to the crowd of people gathered for our benefit. I had to admit that while I might never be the person I was before my "incident," I was a person my NYPD-detective self would have envied.

"You two look so great together," Grandma's friend Mabel said, beaming at us.

"Thank you," we said in unison.

I could smell delicious food in the air, plenty of wine was being poured, and if I didn't know better, I'd almost think we were back in time at Grandma's birthday party. But we weren't; this was our party.

"Congratulations," Sheriff Baker said, coming up to us and shaking Lukas's hand.

Lukas grinned. "I know… I'm a lucky man."

"Yes," I confirmed. "And don't you forget it."

Lukas and I weaved through the crowd, accepting the congratulations, well-wishes, and jokes from what seemed like half the town. Everyone asked to see the ring, and I was pleased to show it off. Lukas had retrieved his mother's sapphire engagement ring, a family heirloom, after the fire had burned down his house. Lukas had worked with a local jeweler to customize my engagement ring, so, along with the sapphires were diamonds from my mother's ring and a ruby from Grandma's engagement ring. I couldn't think of a better way to honor the women who had brought Lukas and me together.

Lukas and I finally got to the buffet table, making sure the kids who'd come from the joint sheriff's and fire departments' youth program didn't sneak a drink of alcohol. I kept smiling until I was sure my cheeks would split. *Damn. I'm so happy.* I was going to marry a man I adored just as much as he loved me.

I heard the telltale opening notes of "our" song, and Lukas didn't have to say a word. We moved as one onto the makeshift dance floor right away, and we danced the way we had at our prom, the way we had at Grandma's birthday. My leg twinged a bit but not enough to make me want to stop.

"You know that we will need something flashier for our first dance as husband and wife," Lukas told me.

"We have plenty of time to work on that," I replied. "We're not getting married for six months."

"That's not a lot of time for a six-foot-four German white boy with no rhythm," Lukas pointed out.

"You have plenty of rhythm," I countered. "Where it counts —in the bedroom," I finished with a saucy smile.

"Ain't that the truth," he said, giving me a soft, lingering kiss before pulling away.

We left the floor when the song changed, and we got something to drink. The party wore on, and I took a break from being on my feet, sitting with Grandma and chatting with her friends while some firefighters took Lukas off for a round of vodka shots.

Something exploded. I didn't know what it was, but the noise sent the surge of adrenaline through my body, and I rose to my feet. Fireworks didn't bother me as much—I could tell the difference—but sudden noises still caught me off guard from time to time. I felt the familiar, dreadful sensation of a flashback, but before I could even look for him, Lukas was at my side, holding my hand tightly.

"Let's slip away," Lukas suggested.

Somehow, we got away from the party and into the country club. Lukas steered me toward a closet.

"Uh, what are you doing?" I asked.

"Trust me," he insisted while getting the door open and me through it. He held me tightly in the dark, stroking my hair until my body relaxed and I started to come back to myself.

"I'm getting better at this," I whispered. Lukas's body shifted against mine.

"Give yourself more credit, Kendra. You're getting amazing at this."

Wrapping my arms around his waist, I breathed in his clean, comforting scent.

"You know," I started. "I've never had sex in a closet."

Lukas laughed. "Do you really want me to get you off in this closet?"

"I'm just saying…I'm willing if you're game," I told him.

Lukas tilted my face up, and despite the lack of light, his lips found mine right away. I melted into his kiss, and I knew he would try his level best to give me a quick orgasm.

"Make sure you keep quiet," Lukas said, pulling me down to the floor.

Straddling his waist, I grinned down at him. "I'm not making any promises," I told him. "It's too hard to keep quiet when you're hitting my kitty just right," I joked.

Lukas growled, rolling over and pinning me under his body.

"Well, if that's a crime, then arrest me right now, Deputy Sheriff Powell."

"Behave, kinky Lukas. Behave…"

* * *

Thank you for reading **HEART OF FIRE!**
 **For more Interracial Romance goodness grab IRRE-SISTIBLE DESIRES!**

**GET A FREE SEDONA VENEZ BOOK!**

https://sedonavenez.com/free-book

# WANT FREE SEDONA VENEZ BOOKS?

Sign up for Sedona Venez's Newsletter and receive FREE BOOKS. In addition to the free stories, you will also get special pricing, exclusive previews and news of new releases.

**GET A FREE SEDONA VENEZ BOOK!**

Join Sedona's mailing list to be the first to know of new releases, free books, special prices and other author giveaways.

https://sedonavenez.com/free-book

# ABOUT THE AUTHOR

USA TODAY BESTSELLING AUTHOR SEDONA VENEZ lives in New York City with her hot ex-military hubby—hooah—and their fur babies. She loves writing sizzling, sexy intricate stories about strong but broken characters who push limits, overcome their fears and risk it all for love.

*Sedona loves to connect with readers!*
www.sedonavenez.com